Praise for Vicki Lewis Thompson

"It's a wonderful sexy romance, with some very appealing and likable characters, and I'm definitely going to delve into more of the Thunder Mountain Brotherhood series."
—*HarlequinJunkie*, Top Pick, on *Cowboy Untamed*

"The tongue-in-cheek, sweet yet sensual and comfortable family feel...remains until the last page. *Cowboy After Dark* is a story that will keep you smiling."
—*RT Book Reviews*, Top Pick

"Thompson continues to do what she does best, tying together strong family values bound by blood and choice, interspersed with the more sizzling aspects of the relationship."
—*RT Book Reviews* on *Thunderstruck*

"All the characters, background stories and character development are positively stellar; the warm family feeling is not saccharine-sweet, but heartfelt and genuine, and Lexi and Cade's rekindled romance is believable from beginning to end, along with the classy, sexy and tender love scenes."
—*Fresh Fiction* on *Midnight Thunder*

"Vicki Lewis Thompson has compiled a tale of this terrific family, along with their friends and employees, to keep you glued to the page and ending with that warr
—*Fresh F*

D1397399

Dear Reader,

It's the middle of the summer at Thunder Mountain Ranch, and that means summer storms! I live close to the mountains, too, and I've experienced the majesty of towering, blue-black clouds, blinding flashes of lightning and thunder that rattles the windows. I've been caught in sheets of rain that soaked me to the skin.

That's the kind of weather Zeke Rafferty and Tess Irwin are forced to deal with. It's the perfect backdrop for two passionate people at cross-purposes, and I can't wait for you to dive into their story! Like all members of the Thunder Mountain Brotherhood, Zeke battles his demons. Unlike his foster brothers, he's never allowed himself to count on the security he found at Thunder Mountain with foster parents Rosie and Herb Padgett. He's remained a lone wolf, but now his protective shell is cracking under the weight of circumstances he can't control.

As Tess and Zeke's story unfolds, you'll have a chance to catch up with Rosie and peek in on little Sophie, Rosie's first grandchild. You'll also be able to watch Sophie work her magic on Zeke. Nothing like a little redheaded moppet to turn a tough cowboy into a softie.

Now that you're here, grab a seat in one of the Adirondack chairs on the front porch at Thunder Mountain and watch the storm clouds roll in. Rosie's sure to bring you a cup of coffee and catch you up on the latest news. If you're a newcomer, don't worry. You'll feel right at home in no time!

Stormily yours,

Vicki Lewis Thompson

Say Yes
to the Cowboy

———

Vicki Lewis Thompson

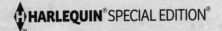
HARLEQUIN® SPECIAL EDITION®

If you purchased this book without a cover you should be aware that this book is stolen property. It was reported as "unsold and destroyed" to the publisher, and neither the author nor the publisher has received any payment for this "stripped book."

Recycling programs
for this product may
not exist in your area.

ISBN-13: 978-0-373-62358-7

Say Yes to the Cowboy

Copyright © 2017 by Vicki Lewis Thompson

All rights reserved. Except for use in any review, the reproduction or utilization of this work in whole or in part in any form by any electronic, mechanical or other means, now known or hereinafter invented, including xerography, photocopying and recording, or in any information storage or retrieval system, is forbidden without the written permission of the publisher, Harlequin Enterprises Limited, 225 Duncan Mill Road, Don Mills, Ontario M3B 3K9, Canada.

This is a work of fiction. Names, characters, places and incidents are either the product of the author's imagination or are used fictitiously, and any resemblance to actual persons, living or dead, business establishments, events or locales is entirely coincidental.

This edition published by arrangement with Harlequin Books S.A.

For questions and comments about the quality of this book, please contact us at CustomerService@Harlequin.com.

® and TM are trademarks of Harlequin Enterprises Limited or its corporate affiliates. Trademarks indicated with ® are registered in the United States Patent and Trademark Office, the Canadian Intellectual Property Office and in other countries.

Printed in U.S.A.

A passion for travel has taken *New York Times* bestselling author **Vicki Lewis Thompson** to Europe, Great Britain, the Greek isles, Australia and New Zealand. She's visited most of North America and has her eye on South America's rain forests. Africa, India and China beckon. But her first love is her home state of Arizona, with its deserts, mountains, sunsets and—last but not least—cowboys! The wide-open spaces and heroes on horseback influence everything she writes. Connect with her at vickilewisthompson.com, Facebook.com/vickilewisthompson and Twitter.com/vickilthompson.

Books by Vicki Lewis Thompson

Harlequin Special Edition

Thunder Mountain Brotherhood

In the Cowboy's Arms

Harlequin Blaze

Thunder Mountain Brotherhood

Midnight Thunder
Thunderstruck
Rolling Like Thunder
A Cowboy Under the Mistletoe
Cowboy All Night
Cowboy After Dark
Cowboy Untamed
Cowboy Unwrapped

Sons of Chance

Cowboys & Angels
Riding High
Riding Hard
Riding Home
A Last Chance Christmas

Visit the Author Profile page
at Harlequin.com for more titles.

To the many copy editors over the years who've tightened my prose and questioned my word choices. We share the same geeky obsession with language, so it's too bad we can't all meet in the bar for a drink. I know we'd get along!

Chapter One

When a truck drove up outside the ranch house, Zeke Rafferty put down the barbell and grabbed a towel to mop his face. The workout wasn't that hard, but the pain in his shoulder made him sweat like a pig. As he pulled on a T-shirt, the soft cotton stuck to his skin.

He'd recently decided to let his beard grow, so he hoped his visitor was someone who wouldn't mind the sweat or the scruff. Walking out onto the front porch helped cool him off. Maybe he should start doing his exercises there so he could catch the Wyoming evening breeze.

He was glad to see the Thunder Mountain Academy logo on the tan pickup in front of the house. Anyone driving that truck would be family. When he saw it was Rosie, his foster mom, he hurried over to open the door for her. His nose told him she'd baked him a rhubarb pie. Excellent.

"Came over to see how you're doing." She handed him the pie and then waved him off as he started to help her down. "Don't put a strain on your shoulder, son."

"I won't." He got a kick out of seeing her at the wheel of such a massive vehicle. The top of her fluffed-up blond hairdo barely reached his shoulder yet she drove that truck with authority. He transferred the pie to his other hand and used his good arm to steady her as she stepped on the running board and hopped down. "The pie smells great."

"It's still warm. Do you have any of that vanilla ice cream left?"

"Yes, ma'am."

"Then, if you'll make me some decaf, I wouldn't mind a slice before I head back. By the way, Herb said to say hello."

"Thanks." Zeke enjoyed these impromptu visits from his foster parents. He was fine with his own company, which made him the perfect caretaker for his foster brother Matt's ranch, but he didn't mind having someone to talk to now and then.

Maybe his nights seemed especially quiet because his days were filled with the sounds of hammering and sawing, sometimes punctuated with a baby's squeals and laughter. His foster brother Damon Harrison and Damon's wife, Philomena, were renovating the house for Matt, and they usually brought along their seven-month-old baby, Sophie. Zeke wasn't much help with the renovation because of his shoulder, so he entertained Sophie when she was awake.

Rosie glanced at the sawhorses in the living room

and the cartons of hardwood flooring. "Damon mentioned that they'd decided to replace the floors in all the bedrooms."

"Yes, ma'am, and it'll be beautiful when they're done. Matt's gonna love it."

"He will. They do fabulous work. Speaking of Matt, have you heard from him recently?" Rosie headed for the kitchen.

"He called this morning." Zeke started on the coffee. "Wanted to warn me that he'd ordered a kitchen table and chairs." He gestured at the card table and folding chairs in the room now. "Should be here in a few days." After landing a starring role in a Western being released in September, Matt was on track to become the most famous of the Thunder Mountain foster boys. With his improved finances, he'd bought this place, outside Sheridan and adjacent to Thunder Mountain Ranch. Matt's timing had been perfect for Zeke. A torn rotator cuff from years of trick roping had forced him to leave the rodeo circuit for a few months. Keeping an eye on Matt's property and overseeing renovations and furniture delivery had given him a spot to land until he healed.

"You're going to the premiere, right?" Rosie put generous servings of pie on two plates and added a scoop of ice cream to each. Then she put them on the table along with napkins and forks. She'd helped Zeke organize the kitchen when he'd moved in, so she knew her way around.

"Planning on it."

"How's your shoulder?"

"Better." It was his standard answer but progress was too damned slow. He worried that even after he was healed enough to get back to his routine, he'd need hours of practice before feeling confident he could dazzle the fans.

"I went online today and found a video of you performing at a rodeo in Vegas. Do you always wear sparkly clothes or was that a Vegas thing?"

He laughed. "I always do. I have a closet full of that stuff. When the spotlight hits me, I'm a regular rhinestone cowboy." After adding cream to Rosie's coffee, he brought both mugs to the table.

"I liked the routine in the dark where the ropes light up."

"Those are tricky to work with but they're a crowd-pleaser." He took a seat across from Rosie. "I'm flattered that you looked for the video."

"I had ulterior motives. I wanted to see if the students would go for it, and they definitely would. Once you're healed, I'd love to have you teach a short roping class at the academy if you can work it into your schedule."

He smiled. "Is that why you made my favorite pie?"

"I figured it couldn't hurt."

"I'd be glad to." His temporary move to Matt's place had given him a chance to see Thunder Mountain Academy in action. Years ago Rosie and Herb had sheltered numerous foster boys at their ranch. Then in retirement they'd found themselves with financial problems through no fault of their own.

Some of their foster sons had rallied to help them create Thunder Mountain Academy, a for-credit residential program for older teens where they'd learn everything equine-related. Zeke hadn't kept in touch as much as some of the other guys, so he hadn't heard about the financial crisis until it had been taken care of.

Fortunately the successful program had kept his foster parents from selling the ranch. It also had been a blessing in disguise because they'd obviously been bored once all the foster boys had grown and left. Unlike Zeke, they were extremely social.

"We'd pay you to teach classes in roping," Rosie said.

"Not necessary. I wasn't here to help set up the academy so it's the least I can do." He lifted a forkful of pie. "Just make me a few of these and I'm good. It's hard to find decent rhubarb pie."

"I know. Not enough demand. Until you came along I never made it because nobody else liked it besides me. Having you a short drive away is a bonus for lots of reasons, but I love the excuse to make this pie."

Zeke scooped up another bite. "Happy to be of service."

"Incidentally, someone called today looking for you."

"Who?" He paused, his fork in midair.

"Tess Irwin. She lives in Casper." Rosie gazed at him. "Your ice cream's dripping all over."

"Whoops." He shoved the mixture of pie and melting ice cream into his mouth, which bought him a little time to think.

"I take it you recognize the name." Rosie's blue eyes saw much more than he wanted her to.

"Yes, ma'am. We met in Texas in April. She and her girlfriend came down because her girlfriend's going with one of my buddies on the circuit. So Tess and I… spent time together."

"She gave me her number and asked you to call." Rosie pushed a slip of paper across the table. "I promised to pass it on."

"Thanks." He stuffed the paper into his pocket without looking at it.

Rosie changed the subject to an upcoming wedding at the ranch. Cade Gallagher was the first foster boy Rosie and Herb had taken in. He was marrying Lexi Simmons, his high school sweetheart, in less than a month. Rosie had been waiting for that wedding for a long time and she loved discussing the details. Zeke was glad he'd be here for it.

After Rosie left, he took one of the folding chairs from the kitchen and sat on the front porch. The scent of rain was in the air. It had rained the first night he'd had sex with Tess. He couldn't really call it making love because they'd just met. Rain had beat on the window as they'd undressed each other.

If he closed his eyes, he could picture her perfectly: blond hair down past her shoulders, blue eyes, nice breasts, slim waist, shapely legs. She'd mentioned a divorce the previous year. She hadn't been looking for a steady guy, just someone to have fun with.

She had, in fact, been looking for someone exactly like him, a man with no plans to settle down, a man who could enjoy a couple of nights with her and expect nothing more. When it came to people, he had no expectations. His father had taught him two things— roping and self-reliance. Zeke had become proficient at both.

He'd never expected to see Tess again, yet here she was, tracking him down. She hadn't seemed like the stalker type. In any case, he wouldn't call her back.

He'd come here to heal and take care of Matt's place, at least for the next few months. He wasn't interested in whatever Tess had in mind.

When he went back inside, he took the scrap of paper from his pocket, crumpled it up and tossed it in the trash.

Tess allowed a week to go by before putting in another call to Rosie. Rosie didn't sound happy to hear that Zeke hadn't called. When Tess emphasized the urgency of the matter, Rosie suggested she come in person so they could work things out.

Tess had no idea how they'd do that, but she wasn't in a position to question Rosie. She packed an overnight bag and threw it in her sedan before driving north toward Sheridan. At the turnoff to the ranch, she saw a wooden sign announcing it as the location of Thunder Mountain Academy.

The ranch itself had a homey feel. An old-fashioned, hip-roofed barn was off to the left and the low-slung house sported an awesome front porch that ran the length of the building. Adirondack chairs in alternating brown and green lined the porch. The sign she'd seen initially was painted in the same colors, which must have something to do with the academy, whatever that was.

A short, blond woman who might be in her sixties came through the front door and stood on the porch as Tess climbed out of her car.

"Tess?" she called as she walked down the steps.

"Yes, that's me. Are you Rosie?"

"I am."

"Is Zeke here?" All the way from Casper she'd wondered if she'd step inside the ranch house and find him waiting for her.

"Not yet, but I've invited him for dinner."

"Does he know that I'll be here?"

"No."

Tess's stomach churned with anxiety. "I appreciate what you're trying to do, but I don't want to ambush him."

"Tess, he's deliberately avoiding you, and I didn't raise that boy to be rude, especially to a young lady he has a connection to. I intend to make sure that you get a chance to talk with him."

"You're his mother?" If this petite, plump and fair-skinned woman had given birth to Zeke, he must take after his dad.

"Foster mother."

"Oh! Oh, my goodness. He never told me that he'd been in foster care."

"That doesn't surprise me. Listen, why don't you get your bag and come inside for some lemonade and peanut butter cookies?"

"Okay. Thank you." Tess let out a breath. Rosie's blue-eyed gaze was kind, and kindness was welcome right now. Lemonade and cookies sounded pretty darned good, too.

After depositing her overnight bag in a guest room, she sat at Rosie's kitchen table, enjoying her snack while Rosie filled her in on the history of Thunder Mountain. Then Rosie explained the structure of the academy and why it existed.

Tess hung on every word. Knowing that Zeke had been a foster child added a new challenge to the situation. But every bit of information helped, including the tidbit Rosie had provided about his injured shoulder.

"He's terrific. A great guy," Rosie said. "But he's always held himself apart from the rest of us. I won't divulge his past. That's for him to reveal if he chooses to. But I won't kid you…he has issues. Even though I don't approve of his decision not to call you, I understand why he might not. His bum shoulder has turned him into an injured bear hiding in a cave."

"I can see him doing that. He's so independent. I'll bet not being able to work drives him nuts."

"I'm sure it does. But I taught my boys manners. He should have given you the courtesy of contacting you and listening to whatever it is you have to say."

Tess smiled. She really liked this woman. "But you could have insisted he call me back instead of inviting me up here."

"Wouldn't you rather see him in person?"

"Yes. Yes, I would."

Rosie laid a hand on hers. "Zeke won't be here for another hour. Maybe you'd like to have a little rest before he gets here."

She knows. Tess could see it in her eyes. "Is he close by?"

"In Wyoming terms, we're neighbors. He's agreed to be the caretaker at his brother's ranch while he's healing his shoulder."

Tess pushed back her chair and picked up her empty lemonade glass. "I'm going to take you up on that suggestion of resting before dinner. Unless you need help?"

"Thank you, but I have it covered. The students are in charge of making their own dinner tonight and

I have meat loaf and scalloped potatoes ready to pop in the oven for the family."

Tess's mouth watered. Food was one of her obsessions these days, and eating someone else's cooking would be a treat. "That sounds delicious."

"I'll tap on your door when he gets here."

"All right." A surge of anxiety canceled her hunger. "Thank you."

Tess escaped to her bedroom, which was decorated in soothing tones of green. Kicking off her shoes, she stretched out on the bed and launched into the deep breathing exercises she'd been practicing.

That helped. Starting at the top of her head, she gradually relaxed her entire body. Outside her window a bird sang a cheerful little song, but otherwise the house was quiet. Peaceful. It was, she could tell, a good house. A refuge.

Chapter Two

After what seemed like five minutes, Rosie tapped on her door. "Tess, he's here."

Heart pounding and palms sweating, Tess brushed her hair, refreshed her makeup and smoothed the wrinkles from her blouse and slacks. As she was about to open the door, she heard Zeke's deep laugh. She hadn't thought she'd remember it, but the sound awakened feelings she'd hoped she'd buried. She didn't want to be attracted to him—not anymore—but her libido seemed to have other ideas.

She heard another man chuckle. That must be Herb, Rosie's husband. Rosie had mentioned he would be the only other person there for dinner. Sometimes there was a crowd, she'd said, but not tonight. Tess figured that was on purpose.

When she walked into the living room, Zeke was

sitting on one end of the sofa, holding a bottle of beer. A wiry older man, undoubtedly Herb, had taken the opposite end and Rosie was in a comfy-looking armchair. Both men popped up immediately.

Herb smiled in welcome, but Zeke's face, what she could see of it since he now had a full beard and wore his Stetson, was brick-red with either anger or embarrassment. Maybe both.

He gave Rosie a quick what-the-hell glance before turning back to her. "Hello, Tess." He cleared his throat. "Wasn't expecting you."

"I invited her." Rosie stood. "Tess, this is my husband, Herb."

"Nice meeting you." Herb walked over and shook her hand. "Glad you could pay us a visit." He, too, had kind eyes.

"Thank you." She managed a smile. "So am I. Your place is charming."

"Dinner will be ready in about fifteen minutes," Rosie said, "but I can let it simmer a little longer if you two need more time to talk. Herb, let's go whip up a salad."

"I'm on it." He left the room.

Tess wished she could follow them both into the kitchen. She'd rather do almost anything than stay there with the smoldering volcano that was Zeke. But Rosie was right. Telling him in person was the way to go, no matter how awkward it might turn out to be.

He let out a breath and met her gaze. "Guess I should have called you."

"Maybe this is better."

Gradually the color drained from his face. "Why?"

"I'm pregnant."

He stared at her. Then he shook his head. "You can't be."

"I didn't think it was possible, either, so I put off going to the doctor. Frankly, I thought I might have some serious health issues and I didn't want to deal with them until school was out."

His breathing accelerated. "How can you be pregnant? We used condoms!"

"I can't answer that for sure. The doctor said it could be for any number of reasons, but she said it happens."

"So much for modern science." He grimaced. "Look, this feels like a lousy thing to say, but I have to ask. Are you sure it was me?"

"That's a fair question. But you were my first lover after my divorce, which was a year ago, and there's been nobody since. I don't have any proof, though, so you'll have to take my word for it."

"I will."

"Thank you." That was one ugly discussion they could skip. "Look, I know this is a shock, but let me put your mind to rest. I'm here to inform you because I don't believe in keeping a pregnancy a secret from the father, but I don't expect anything from you."

"But you're pregnant with my kid!"

She shrugged. "So what? You didn't intend for this to happen and, judging from our discussions in April, you never planned to have children, so I'll handle everything. I absolve you of any responsibility."

"That's crazy. You can't just—"

"Sure I can. I'll have a lawyer draw up something legal for us to sign if you'd prefer that. I know you don't want him, but the thing is, I do. I love children, but I was told I had about a five percent chance of ever conceiving. This is a miracle baby and I can't wait to be a mother."

"You said *him*."

"Yes. I'm having a boy."

"I thought you couldn't tell at three months."

"They have a blood test now. It's very accurate."

He rubbed a hand over his face. "A boy. Wow." Then he glanced toward the kitchen. "Did you tell Rosie you were pregnant? Is that why she set up this meeting?"

"No, you're the first person I've told."

"Really? What about your folks? What about your friend, the one you came to Texas with?"

"Nobody knows. I wanted a plan before I broke the news. But I think Rosie suspects. When I called back a second time and told her it was very important that I get in touch with you, she probably guessed why."

"I should have called. I apologize for that. I thought—well, it doesn't matter. I still should've called."

"You thought I was out of school and looking for a way to spice up my summer?"

"Yes, ma'am, I did." His hazel eyes gleamed for a moment but then the twinkle was gone. "And I'm not feeling up to that."

The temporary gleam of desire got to her. She hated to admit it, but the longer they talked, the more she wanted to touch him. "I'm sorry about your shoulder. I thought you might show up here in a sling." She didn't know which shoulder was injured, either.

"I have one but I don't like wearing it."

"Does your bad shoulder make it hard to shave?"

"Shave? No, I'm right-handed. Oh." He stroked his

beard. "You mean this. I decided to grow it since I'm not doing public appearances."

"Mmm." She wondered if it would be prickly or soft.

"You don't like it."

"It makes you look different." Like a pirate or a mountain man, both intimidating images of rugged men who couldn't be bothered with changing diapers and warming bottles.

"You don't look different." His gaze drifted to her stomach. "This is so hard to believe. I feel like this is a dream and any minute I'll wake up."

"Trust me, I felt the same when I got the news. The difference is, I was thrilled. I don't expect you to be."

"I don't know what I'm feeling, Tess." He looked into her eyes. "I'm pretty disoriented right now."

"That's understandable."

Rosie appeared in the doorway. "Dinner's ready. But you don't have to come right away if you need more time."

"I do need some time." Zeke glanced her way. "I wouldn't be fit company right now, anyway. If you'll excuse me, I'll take a rain check on dinner."

"Your decision, but I made another rhubarb pie."

"Thanks, Rosie. At least I know you're not too mad at me for not returning Tess's call."

"I wasn't mad, son. Just a little disappointed. If you feel the need to head on back, I'll save some of the pie for another time."

"That would be great." Crossing the room in three long strides, he gave her a quick kiss on the cheek. "And thanks for setting me straight on this deal."

"You're welcome."

He turned back to Tess. "I'd like to ask a favor, if I may?"

"What's that?"

"I'd appreciate it if you'd stick around for another day or so. Give me a chance to get my bearings before you go back to Casper."

"I don't want to impose on your foster parents."

"It's not an imposition," Rosie said. "Stay as long as you like."

Zeke nodded. "Good, then. It's settled. I'll be back tomorrow. Ladies." Touching the brim of his hat, he walked out the front door.

Zeke made the trip back to Matt's ranch on autopilot. He couldn't have said how he got there but, sure enough, there he was parked in front of the house. He sat in the truck for a while, unable to summon the energy to go inside.

Against all odds, he'd created a child, something he'd vowed never to do. Worse yet, the kid was a boy. He'd decided years ago that girls were more resilient. They bonded with each other in some mysterious way that strengthened them against disaster.

But a boy—specifically *his* boy—could end up battling demons alone. That had certainly been Zeke's experience. And when this as-yet-unnamed boy figured out that his father had abandoned all parental responsibility? Guaranteed he'd have demons.

Eventually, Zeke climbed out of his truck, went into the house and stripped off his good shirt so he could do his exercises. And because he lost track of his repetitions, he ended up in more pain than usual. He bypassed his prescription pain medication in favor of a beer.

Sitting on the front porch on one of the folding chairs, he drank the beer and contemplated his options. He didn't have a lot of them, and none were part of the life he'd imagined. But as the beer mellowed him out, he allowed his thoughts to dwell on Tess.

She was beautiful, way prettier than he'd remembered. He'd heard that pregnancy gave women a special glow. It might be true because she'd seemed lit from within. Her eagerness to have this baby was appealing. Hell, it was more than that. Her enthusiasm about bringing a new life into this world turned him on.

Yeah, there it was. The naked truth. Tess had been a great lover, and he had fond memories of their time in that Texas hotel room. But Tess as the mother of his child transformed her into a woman of irresistible appeal. If the attraction he'd felt back in April could be compared to a backyard fountain, this new emotion was more like Niagara Falls.

He wondered if his reaction was connected to some primitive urge to claim the female who'd successfully welcomed his bid for immortality. He hadn't realized at the time how unlikely this mating had been. Knowing that he'd overcome the condom barrier plus her apparent infertility made him feel…okay, it made him feel like one heck of a stud.

But when he wasn't mentally strutting around like the prize rooster in the henhouse, he was scared spitless. He'd had reasons for avoiding fatherhood and none of them had changed just because he'd accidentally gotten a woman pregnant. He had skeletons in his closet, and Tess had every right to know what they were.

On the other hand, maybe he didn't have to drag out those skeletons in the next twenty-four hours.

* * *

During dinner, Tess broke the news of her pregnancy to Rosie and Herb. That's when she learned that Rosie considered the unborn baby her future grandchild.

"I realize that's slightly unconventional." She passed Tess a basket of warm yeast rolls. "But most of those boys call us Mom and Dad, so why not? Babies need grandparents to spoil them rotten."

Tess laughed, charmed by the prospect of Rosie and Herb as her son's grandparents. "I suppose they do. Mine treated me like a princess. I came along after they'd given up on having any, so I really did get spoiled. I'm sad that they're gone now. They would have loved fussing over another baby."

"Of course they would! Sophie—that's Damon and Phil's daughter—is the light of my life. She'll be a year by the time your little guy is born. That's old enough for her to understand that she has a new baby cousin. I can't wait to see them together. It'll be adorable."

"Yes, well…" Tess had allowed herself to get carried away by Rosie's enthusiasm. "I'm not sure how often I'll get over here. I'll do my best but…"

"Oh." Rosie shared a quick glance with Herb. "You'll have to excuse me, Tess. I was so focused on the baby that I didn't think about anything else. Zeke will be back on the circuit by then, not living next door. I shouldn't make assumptions about how the two of you will work everything out. For all I know, you're going to travel with him."

She shuddered at the thought. "I plan to raise the baby on my own."

Rosie gave a little gasp of surprise. "Does Zeke know?"

"I told him tonight."

Herb frowned. "And what did he say?"

"Not much. But when we met he told me he didn't want kids. In my opinion, a reluctant father is worse than no father at all."

Herb's frown deepened. "But Zeke has a financial obligation to his son."

She met Herb's worried gaze. "Legally, yes, but I'm relieving him of that. I'm financially capable of raising this child and, despite my right to child support, I couldn't in good conscience take money from a man who won't be participating in the process."

Rosie and Herb greeted that statement with a long silence. Tess wished circumstances could be different for these two wonderful people. But this baby was a gift and she refused to let him become an obligation to anyone, least of all the man who'd unintentionally fathered him.

Finally, Rosie took a deep breath. "I can understand why you feel that way. But we'd love to be part of the process, so I hope you'll bring that sweet baby over to see us now and then."

"I will." She reached over and squeezed Rosie's arm. "I promise."

After that, Rosie demonstrated her conversational skills, because the baby and Zeke weren't mentioned again. Tess's admiration for Rosie's social abilities grew as they spent the rest of the meal discussing various teaching methods. They talked about the differences and similarities between Tess's primary students and the teens that Rosie and Herb had worked with, both as foster parents and founders of Thunder Mountain Academy.

Immersed in her favorite subject, Tess lost track of time as they lingered over dessert. Rosie had made two pies: rhubarb and cherry. Herb was the only one eating the cherry pie as Tess and Rosie each enjoyed a generous slice of the rhubarb topped with vanilla ice cream. Judging from Rosie's comment to Zeke before he left, he was a fan of this particular flavor, too. But Rosie never brought it up.

Tess helped with the dishes before bidding Rosie and Herb good-night. She was touched by their willingness to accept whatever plan she had for this baby. Her own parents weren't likely to react the same way and she dreaded the confrontation when she told them. But she didn't have to worry about that tonight.

After a satisfying meal with two people who made her feel at home, she was more than ready for a good night's sleep. Her last thought was of Zeke's full beard. In a way, it helped that he'd grown one because he looked so different from the man she'd tumbled into bed with back in April. She could more easily pretend he was a stranger, one she would never see again after tomorrow.

Chapter Three

Zeke woke at dawn. Early morning light filtered through the leaves of a tree outside the window and he enjoyed watching the patterns created on the west wall. Once Damon and Phil had installed new flooring in the two smaller bedrooms, he'd move into one of them. He'd be sorry to leave the master bedroom, though.

Climbing out of bed, he headed into the bathroom. He rummaged in his shaving kit for a pair of manicure scissors and clipped off most of his beard. Then he took a razor to what was left.

A hot shower relieved some of the tension in his neck and shoulders, but it came back the minute he dried off. He dressed in his nicest shirt and jeans, and polished his boots. His hat got a good brushing, too. He'd let it get dusty and that wouldn't do for what he had in mind.

Damon and Phil would arrive in a couple of hours with little Sophie, but they'd have to manage the baby without his help. He wrote them a quick note explaining that he had an errand to run at Thunder Mountain and couldn't be sure when he'd be back. If all went well, he might be gone all day.

Grabbing his keys, he locked up the house and walked out to his truck. It could use a wash, but he didn't have the time. He used his hand to clean off the passenger seat before walking around to the driver's side and sliding in behind the wheel.

On the way to Thunder Mountain, he had the same feeling in the pit of his stomach that he always got right before he stepped into the arena for a performance. So he followed the same technique and, several deep breaths later, he was calmer.

The academy kids were busy down at the barn taking care of morning chores when he pulled up in front of the house. He saw Cade and Herb with them, supervising. Cade looked up and waved. By now he probably knew the score. Herb would have filled him in.

Zeke lifted a hand in acknowledgment before mounting the steps to the porch. He rapped on the screen door and opened it while calling out a greeting. For anyone who'd lived at the ranch, that was all Rosie and Herb required. The door was nearly always open for their family.

Zeke had never let himself fully accept being a part of Herb and Rosie's family. Counting on something to stay the same was a recipe for disappointment. While the other guys called Rosie and Herb "Mom and Dad," he didn't. They referred to the ranch as "home" but he hadn't made the mistake of labeling it that way. Even so, he enjoyed the privilege of walking into the house whenever he wanted.

"In the kitchen!" Rosie responded.

He found her predictable breakfast routine a comfort, but he'd never taken that for granted, either. He could tell some of the other guys did.

When he walked into the kitchen, it was just Rosie and Sharon, the cook they'd hired to help fix meals for the academy students. She was a middle-aged lady with short brown hair and a great laugh. No Tess.

"Hey, Zeke." Rosie turned from the stove to look at him. "Where's your beard?"

"Shaved it off." He glanced over at Sharon and touched the brim of his hat. "Howdy, ma'am."

"Howdy, Zeke. I was growing partial to that beard."

"It was starting to itch. Can I help you two with anything?"

Rosie handed him a bowl and a whisk. "You can scramble these eggs. Sharon and I have already delivered the food to the rec hall, so she's ready to leave. Herb will be back from the barn shortly."

"See you two later." The cook grabbed her tote bag out of the storeroom.

"Bye, Sharon," Rosie said. "Thanks!"

Zeke waited until she went out the front door. "Tess isn't up yet?"

"Not yet." Rosie eyed him. "You can start scrambling those eggs anytime now."

"Yes, ma'am." He set the bowl on the counter and started in on them. "She told you, right?"

"She did. And you'd better give me those eggs before you beat them to death."

He handed over the bowl and Rosie poured the

mixture into the frying pan. Bacon sizzled in another pan and country fries were cooking away in a third. Normally he'd be salivating for one of Rosie's famous breakfasts, but he wasn't even slightly hungry.

"Zeke, please don't pace."

"Sorry." He hadn't realized he was doing it.

"Would you like some coffee?"

"No, thank you, ma'am."

"Well, I would, so please pour me a cup and sit down at the table. I'll be there in a minute."

"Yes, ma'am." He got her coffee, carried it to the table and took a seat.

She turned down the heat under each of the pans and covered them with lids. As she approached the table, Zeke stood and held her chair for her.

"Thank you." She settled herself and wrapped both hands around her coffee mug. "I take it you have a plan."

"Yes, ma'am."

"Judging from how spiffy you look, I can guess what it is, but I should probably warn you that—"

"Good morning." Tess walked into the room wearing a soft blue button-up shirt and jeans.

Zeke leaped to his feet again and knocked over his chair. "Good morning." He righted the chair and gazed at her. She looked incredible. Her hair shone like gold and her cheeks were flushed as if she might be as nervous about their situation as he was.

She stared at him. "What happened to your beard?"

"It itched, so I shaved it off."

"Oh."

"Hail, hail, the gang's all here." Herb walked into the kitchen. "I can't speak for anyone else, but I'm starving." He took plates from a cupboard. "I vote we serve ourselves from the stove."

Rosie stood. "That works. I'll make us some toast. Zeke, you can get out the silverware and napkins. Tess, coffee mugs are in the cabinet nearest the window, first shelf. I have mine but we'll need three more."

Zeke had thought about lying and saying he'd had breakfast before he'd come over, but he was a lousy liar and Rosie wouldn't believe him anyway. Nobody in his right mind ate breakfast beforehand if he had a chance to enjoy Rosie's cooking. He filled his plate and sat with everyone else.

Herb picked up his coffee mug and paused with it halfway to his mouth. "Why did you shave off your beard, Zeke?"

"He said it itched." Rosie gave Herb a glance that said plainly he shouldn't pursue the matter.

Zeke appreciated the intervention on his behalf. He didn't want his beard removal to become the main topic of conversation.

Herb shrugged. "I can see that could be an issue. So, Tess, the kids have cleared out of the pasture area if you'd like to head down there with me or Zeke and take a look at the horses."

That would delay Zeke's plan and the longer he delayed, the more likely he'd lose his nerve. "Actually, I—"

"I'd love to," Tess said. "I wanted one so bad when I was a kid but my parents weren't into horses. Since then I've taken lessons, although I can't claim to be a seasoned rider."

Zeke looked at her in surprise. "I didn't know you ride."

"A little. I'm taking a break from it until the baby's born, just to be on the safe side."

"Good." He sighed in relief. "That's good." He'd been around horses all his life and loved them, but he didn't like the idea of Tess riding one and chancing a fall.

"The advice on riding while pregnant is conflicting," Herb said, "but since it's not something you do on a daily basis, I think you're smart to stop for the next few months."

Tess nodded. "Thanks. But I'd love to visit your horses. How many do you have?"

"Six at the moment." Herb ticked them off on his fingers. "Technically, Lucy and Linus, a palomino mare and her son, don't belong to us. We're boarding them."

Tess smiled. "Love the names."

"Then we have Cade's big black horse, Hematite, and his fiancée Lexi's mare, Serendipity, Serra for short. Finally there's Navarre and Isabeau, my gelding and Rosie's mare."

"You named them after the characters in *Lady-hawke*?"

Now if only he could get Tess to respond with that kind of delight when he had his chance to talk to her. They were burning daylight and his special place looked its best in the morning before that rock heated up.

"Rosie named them," Herb said "She made me watch the movie and, after I did, I agreed to the names. I don't admit this to everyone, but we're all friends here. I'm a sucker for a great romance."

"And that's why I married him." Rosie gazed fondly

at her husband. "He's a stand-up guy, but underneath he's a sentimental sweetie who doesn't mind naming our horses after characters in a love story."

Zeke noticed that Tess was a little misty-eyed. Maybe that was his cue. "Look, I know how much Tess is interested in seeing the horses, but I also wanted to show her the view from Lion's Rest Rock. It's at its best when the sun's at an angle instead of beating straight down."

"Lion's Rest?" Tess gazed at him, her expression difficult to read. "Are you talking about mountain lions?"

"Technically, yes, but if we take the trail up there, I guarantee we won't find one lounging on that flat rock. They'd hear us coming long before we arrived and vamoose."

"But they do hang out there?"

"Sure, when no people are around."

"That's too bad. I'd love to catch a glimpse of one. I never have."

All righty, then. He was quickly learning things about the mother of his child, information that could be valuable in the future. "Well, you never can tell. If we get a move on and walk very quietly up that trail, we might see one disappearing through the underbrush."

He ignored Rosie when she lifted her eyes to the ceiling. So he was exaggerating a little. No one he knew had actually spotted a cougar on that rock. Rumor had it that they perched on it when no people were around because the rock gave them an excellent vantage point for spotting prey. It could be true.

But Lion's Rest Rock was a famous make-out spot because the granite slab was the size of a king mattress, besides being smooth as a well-worn saddle. Zeke couldn't speak for other guys, but he'd never made a conquest up there. His conscience was clear about sharing it with Tess.

Tess finished her coffee and picked up her empty plate. "I'm ready to go see this Lion's Rest Rock, right after we clean up."

"Leave the dishes," Rosie said.

Zeke had never heard more beautiful words in his life. In another forty minutes that rock could be hot as a branding iron. He could get there in ten and lead Tess up the path in another ten. That gave him twenty minutes to execute his plan. It should be enough.

With anticipation vying with anxiety, he ushered Tess out the front door of the ranch house and handed her into the passenger seat of his truck. So far, so good.

"I can't help thinking you have an ulterior motive," she said as he put the truck in gear.

"Why's that?" He didn't dare look at her as he drove. She might see something in his eyes.

"Number one, you shaved off your beard. That had to take a couple of weeks to grow, so why shave it now unless it has something to do with me?"

"My beard grows really fast. It only took about nine days."

"All right, but the timing is still suspicious. Yesterday afternoon you had a bushy beard. Then I tell you I'm pregnant and the next morning you appear with a close shave. Coincidence? I don't think so."

"I got the impression you didn't like it." They reached the paved road and he accelerated.

"I didn't dislike it. I just… What difference does it make, anyway? There's no reason for you to try to please me. We're ships who passed in the night."

"We didn't just pass. We moored in the same spot and produced a dingy."

That gave her the giggles. "I shouldn't have introduced a nautical reference. It makes no sense in Wyoming. We're landlocked."

"Okay, let's compare ourselves to a couple of Conestoga wagons that ended up gathered around the same campfire and produced a little buckboard."

Her laughter was now out of control. "Stop! Don't be funny! This is a very serious situation we're in." But she couldn't seem to keep a straight face.

And it was catching. Soon he was laughing right along with her. When he pulled over onto the side of the road next to the trail leading up to Lion's Rest Rock, he was out of breath. Shutting off the engine, he glanced at her and grinned. "Enough. You'll need both energy and lung power to walk up this trail."

"Is it really that steep?"

"Not too bad, but I can guarantee you one thing. It's more of a challenge while you're laughing."

"Okay. I'll do my best to forget I'm having a little buckboard."

He gazed at her. All that laughter had made her eyes sparkle like sapphires under a high-intensity lamp.

"I assume people hike this trail hoping to spot wildlife."

"Some do, but that's not really what the rock is known for."

Understanding flashed in her eyes and her cheeks turned pink. "Zeke Rafferty, if you think you're going to get me alone up there so we can do *that*, you have another think coming!"

"I don't, I swear! That's the furthest thing from my

mind." Not exactly true, but it was down the list a ways. It didn't rank higher than number three and, considering how pretty she looked, he thought that was damned noble of him.

"So what is on your mind, then?"

"We need to talk, figure stuff out. The view from there is real nice. You can watch the morning shadows move down the mountains as the sun gets higher."

"You seem to know this spot pretty well."

"I do, but not for the reason you're imagining. I used to come up here in the early morning so I could think about things when nobody else was around."

"Come on, Zeke. A guy who looks like you must have had plenty of girlfriends in high school. I can't believe you didn't bring them here to make out."

"You don't have to believe me, but the fact is, I didn't." He opened his door. "It was too special." He hopped down and walked around to her side, but she was already out.

She gazed up at him, her expression tender. "I do believe you. And you're right about the beard. I like you better without it. Lead the way."

He took off before he did something stupid and kissed her. As he climbed, he monitored his pace so he wouldn't wear her out getting to the top.

"You can go faster. I'm in shape. I go for a run every morning."

He turned around so abruptly they almost slammed into each other. "You run? Is that okay?"

"My doctor says it's fine unless I notice any problems after a run. She's in favor of women exercising throughout their pregnancy. It's just the horseback riding she cautioned me about. And the bungee jumping."

His stomach lurched. *"Bungee jumping?"* The mischievous twinkle in her eyes clued him in. "You've never bungee jumped in your life, have you?"

"Nope. Just teasing you."

No kidding. Standing inches away from her, he was teased by a whole bunch of things—the scent of her shampoo, the curve of her cheek and the sound of her breath. He knew the pleasure her kiss could bring and he craved that pleasure again. But he'd promised that wasn't why he'd brought her up there.

"We'd better get a move on." He turned around and started back up the trail. "We want to get there before the sun hits that rock."

Fortunately it was still shaded when they reached the end of the trail. He should have thought to bring a blanket for her to sit on, but then she might have questioned his honorable intentions.

She walked out onto the rock and sucked in a breath. "Gorgeous. Thank you for bringing me up here. Now I wish I'd brought a camera, or at least my phone."

"We can come back another time."

She turned toward him. "No, we can't, Zeke. It'll be better for all three of us if we make a clean break."

"I don't want a clean break." He dropped to one knee. "I don't have a ring to give you, but I'll get one today. Tess Irwin, will you do me the honor of becoming my wife?"

Chapter Four

"Are you crazy?" Tess stared at Zeke in dismay while a voice in her head screeched, *This isn't happening! Dear God, this isn't happening!* "We barely know each other."

His jaw tightened. "We know each other well enough to make a baby. That's a little more intimate than a handshake, Tess. You knew me well enough to get naked with me. Marriages have been built on a lot less."

"But I don't want to be married. I've been there and it wasn't a whole lot of fun. And I thought we were in love! You and I don't even have that going for us."

He rose. "What if that's for the best? What's wrong with getting married for the sake of the kid?"

"*Everything.* In eighteen years or so this baby will be ready to create a life of his own. What then? Will we stay married after he goes off to college or a job in another state? Will we stare at each other across the breakfast table and wonder what the heck we've done to ourselves for the sake of the kid?"

He glanced down at his boots. She noticed they had a light layer of dust on them, though they'd started the walk dust-free. When he looked up again, his gaze was bleak. "I hadn't thought that far ahead."

"But we have to." She should have figured out what he was planning when he appeared this morning in clothes that looked almost new, recently polished boots and a clean-shaved jaw. Yet she'd never dreamed he'd do a complete one-eighty and propose after announcing in April that he'd never marry or have kids. He'd blindsided her because she didn't know him at all.

"Okay, you make a good point about the marriage thing, but I still want to be part of my son's life."

"Why?" She gazed up at him.

"He's my son."

"Look, if you're feeling an obligation because society has conditioned you that way, please try to adjust your thinking. Obligation and duty have no place in this scenario. I won't have someone around this baby who resents him."

"I didn't say I resented him."

"Maybe not yet. He isn't even born. But kids take time away from other things you might want to do and they can be frustrating to deal with sometimes. Considering all you've said about protecting your independent lifestyle, why would you let yourself in for that?"

"Because I want to make sure he'll be okay."

"I promise you that he'll be well taken care of." And

that was the crux of the situation. He didn't trust her to do that. And why should he? He didn't know her, either.

"Tess, I have a legal right to spend time with him."

"I know you do." She felt a stab of panic. "But don't you see? If you're forcing yourself to be a father, that's horrible for a child. They know the difference between love and obligation. You can't fake it, so why even go there?"

"Because he's my *son*."

She sighed. "We're going around in circles. And this rock is getting warmer by the minute. Let's go back."

"But we haven't settled anything."

"I know that." What a maddening man—a gorgeous, stubborn cowboy who still had the power to make her heart beat faster. She doubted he'd spent much time around children, while she'd made a career of it. Zeke had no idea what he would be getting into. Yet, somehow, when he'd dug in his heels and said "He's my son," it turned her on.

She had to watch out for those pesky feelings of lust, though. She'd read enough books on pregnancy to know the hormones coursing through her body could make her susceptible to a virile guy who kept giving her hot glances. He obviously wanted her and that was arousing, but surrendering to those urges would complicate an already dicey situation.

"Are you willing to stick around for another day or two until we come to some kind of agreement on how this will go?"

"I'm willing, but I don't like imposing on your foster parents."

"I seriously doubt they consider it imposing.

Did Rosie give you the word that she loves being a grandma?"

"She did and I think it's sweet. I'm sure she and Herb are terrific grandparents. I'll be happy to keep them in the loop."

His expression darkened. "But not me?"

"You said you didn't want kids, Zeke!"

"That was before I found out you were pregnant. That changes everything."

"It doesn't have to. Just think of yourself as a sperm donor."

"A *sperm donor*?" A dangerous light flashed in his hazel eyes. "Correct me if I'm wrong, but I remember making this baby the old-fashioned way." He stepped closer, his chest heaving. "I distinctly recall having some very sweaty, very satisfying, sex with you, lady, complete with orgasms that made you cry my name so loud I was afraid someone would call hotel security. I was your lover, damn it. I never want to hear that term again."

Heat scorched her body and she clenched her fists at her sides to keep from reaching for him. She swallowed. "Got it."

"And another thing." His voice softened. "Although you don't want to marry me, your eyes tell me what you do want. Just so you know, that would be fine with me, but you'll have to do the asking. Whatever happens or doesn't is your choice." He turned around and started down the trail.

She prayed her legs would carry her as she followed him. He'd snapped her self-control with that speech. If he hadn't turned away, she probably would have launched herself at him and begged for more of that

red-hot loving he'd so graphically described. But he
had turned away and she'd pulled together the pieces
of her shredded pride.

Somehow she'd managed to keep her mouth shut,
but her body still yearned for his touch. She gazed
with longing at his broad shoulders and the movement
of his powerful back muscles. Yes, she was guilty of
ogling, but she'd dare any woman with a pulse to ignore the way his jeans cupped his backside. She'd admired that view on the way up the trail and, after his
impassioned words, she was even more mesmerized
on the way down.

When they reached the truck Zeke handed her in
with brisk efficiency. No significant glances or lingering touches. Apparently he'd meant what he'd said.
Nothing would happen between them unless she initiated it. She vowed not to do that.

After he got behind the wheel, he opened the console and took out his phone. "I'll call Rosie and make
sure she's okay with you staying a little longer."

"All right. Tell her I'd be glad to check into a hotel
in Sheridan, if she prefers."

"Okay." He nudged back his hat and put the phone
to his ear. "Hi, Rosie. Tess needs to stay a few more
days. She's offered to check into a hotel in town." He
smiled. "I know. Yes, ma'am, she's very considerate.
I'll tell her what you said." He disconnected the call
and returned the phone to the console. "You're welcome to stay at the ranch for as long as you want." He
twisted the key in the ignition and the truck's powerful engine roared to life.

"That's nice of her."

"Rosie's great." He checked for traffic and executed

a quick U-turn. "Since I'm the one who set up this discussion, I'll let you call the shots for the next one. Tell me when and where and I'll make sure I'm available."

His self-possession amazed her. She was a bundle of nerves. The combination of his sex appeal and his determination to be a part of the baby's life had torpedoed her original plan. She'd have to create a new plan before she saw him again. "I need a little time. If you'll give me your number I'll text you."

"There's a pad of paper and a pen in the console."

She found them lying inside the compartment. Underneath was a faded brochure advertising "The Ropin' Ragin' Raffertys!" She recognized Zeke, who looked about ten, wearing jeans and a shirt decorated in fringe and spangles. The man beside him in a matching outfit had to be his father.

She closed the console without asking about the brochure. She wished she hadn't seen it. Learning about his past would only draw her deeper into his life and make it harder to extricate herself. She was going to raise her baby on her own. She still believed that would be best for everyone concerned.

Zeke rattled off his phone number. She scribbled it down, tore out the page and returned the pad and pen to the console without looking at the brochure. He'd probably forgotten it was in there. She doubted he was any more eager to share details of his past than she was to hear them.

A truck with a camper shell was parked in the circular gravel drive of the ranch house. Zeke stopped behind it and switched off the engine. "Drew's here."

"Another foster brother?"

He shook his head as he reached for the door handle. "She's a videographer. Cade and Lexi hired her for the wedding." He glanced over at her. "Hang on. I'll help you down."

Tess put a hand on his arm. "That's not necessary." The muscles in his forearm tensed and she removed her hand as if she'd touched a hot stove. "I can get out by myself."

"I know you can." He opened his door. "But that's not how cowboys do things."

Back in April his chivalry had been one of the reasons she'd invited him to her hotel room. She'd had a hunch that he'd know how to treat a woman, and wow, had she been right. Now she wished he'd stop because his manners reminded her of how considerate he could be when they were alone and naked.

But refusing to let him help her in and out of his truck would be petty and pointless. He wasn't using the gallant gesture as an excuse to steal a kiss or a caress. His assistance was proper and impersonal. He didn't even smile.

She turned toward him. "I'll text you this afternoon." That should give her enough time to create a new plan.

"All right. I might run some errands today but I'll take my phone."

"Sounds good. Thanks for showing me Lion's Rest Rock. It's beautiful up there."

An emotion flickered briefly in his eyes. "You're welcome." He touched the tips of his fingers to the brim of his hat. "My pleasure." He turned and walked back around his truck.

His pleasure? Really? She'd shot down his proposal. That couldn't have felt very good. But if she'd hurt him, he wasn't showing any signs of it. He'd only reacted emotionally when she'd suggested he think of himself as a sperm donor.

That had been insensitive of her. Now that she was more in command of herself, she needed to apologize. But he'd already put the truck in gear and driven away.

She'd see him again later today so she could mention it then. On the other hand, if she brought up the heated exchange on the rock, that would refocus attention on their sexual past. Not a good idea.

As she climbed the porch steps and walked toward the door, she wondered about protocol. She was a houseguest and could probably walk in. But instead she rapped on the screen door and called out, "I'm back!" as she opened it.

"We're in the kitchen!" Rosie sounded excited. "Come and tell us whether our idea is crazy or not."

Tess walked in and discovered Rosie and two women, one with her dark hair pulled back in a ponytail and the other with a mop of short brown hair. The one with short hair turned out to be Lexi, Cade's fiancée. The other was Drew Martinelli, the videographer.

Rosie's face was pink with excitement. "We're thinking of having the ceremony in the barn. Is that completely nuts or completely brilliant?"

"I vote for brilliant," Drew said. "I filmed the inside of the barn when I made the promotional video for Thunder Mountain Academy last month and the interior is suffused with a golden light, probably because of all the wood surfaces."

Tess pulled up a chair. "I haven't seen the inside of the barn yet, but it sounds like a fun idea. Would there be room for your guests?"

Lexi pushed over a yellow legal pad where she'd drawn a diagram. "This isn't quite to scale, but it's close. Rosie and I know that barn pretty well, and we think we can fit between thirty and forty people in there, especially if we use benches instead of chairs."

"And we'll gain extra space if we have all the Thunder Mountain Brotherhood standing here in a semicircle behind Cade and Lexi." Rosie pointed to a spot at the front of the barn.

Tess glanced at Rosie in confusion. "What's the Thunder Mountain Brotherhood?"

"Zeke never mentioned it?" Rosie frowned. "Come to think of it, he might not realize he's automatically in. That's a recent development."

"It is," Lexi said. "And I'll bet nobody thought to tell him."

Rosie looked over at Tess. "Sorry, you must have no idea what we're talking about."

"Not a clue."

"Years ago, the first three boys we brought to the ranch declared themselves blood brothers. Secret ceremony in the woods at midnight, pressing bloody palms together, the works."

Tess smiled. "Sounds like it wasn't a secret to you."

"Nothing's a secret to Rosie." Lexi gave her a fond glance. "But she let them think it was. They kept their group exclusive until last year when they figured out that was elitist nonsense and all the guys who'd ever lived here should be members. I need to have Cade talk to Zeke."

"Damon might have more opportunity now that he's over at Matt's so much," Rosie said. "He's one of the original three. In any case, when all my boys are standing up there, Zeke should be with them."

"It'll be a great visual, all those cowboys in a half circle behind the bride and groom," Drew said. "How many men are we talking about?"

Rosie ticked them off on her fingers. "Zeke would make nine. Lexi, I just heard from Austin, who says he's flying home from New Zealand for the wedding. He put his RSVP in the mail but he'll probably get here before it does."

"Junior's coming?" Lexi smiled. "Tess, you'll love him. He was the youngest boy to come to the ranch, only nine when he arrived, so the older kids nicknamed him Junior, which I think he pretty much hates but he puts up with it. Oh, and before I forget…" She reached into a tote bag beside her chair and pulled out an envelope. "Here's your invitation. I wasn't sure whether I'd catch you today but I brought it so I could leave it with Rosie. I hope you can come."

Tess gazed down at the hand-lettered envelope and her throat tightened with emotion. Lexi must have addressed the invitation this morning after hearing from Rosie. "This is incredibly sweet, but I can tell seating will be limited so you don't have to invite me."

"We want you there." Lexi reached over and squeezed her arm. "No matter what happens with Zeke, you're part of the family now."

She swallowed. "Thank you. Then I'll come."

"Good! We'll—"

Drew's phone chimed and she quickly glanced at it. "Sorry, but I have to run. That's my next appointment." She pushed back her chair. "I love the barn idea. Text me and we'll set a time to go down there and finalize the details." She picked up a large backpack. "Nice meeting you, Tess!"

"Same here, Drew." Once she was out the door, Tess gazed at Rosie and Lexi. "If I'm coming to the wedding, then I need to tell you what happened this morning."

Rosie groaned. "I'll bet I know."

"Zeke proposed."

Although Lexi gasped, Rosie nodded as if she'd expected that news. She wasn't smiling in anticipation, either. "What did you say?"

"The only thing I could say. I can't marry a man I barely know just because I'm pregnant with his child."

"Of course you can't." Rosie shook her head and sighed. "I could tell when he walked in the kitchen this morning that he'd decided to do something stupid." She looked over at Lexi. "He even shaved off his beard for the occasion."

Lexi rolled her eyes. "What an idiot."

"I still want to come to the wedding," Tess said, "but I can't guarantee how well Zeke and I will be getting along at that point. Unfortunately, I think he proposed because he doesn't trust me to raise this baby."

"No, he probably doesn't." Rosie gave her a warm smile. "But I do."

Chapter Five

Damon and Phil's truck was in the drive when Zeke came back to Matt's ranch. He wondered if either of them had talked to Rosie yet. If not, then he'd be the one to give them the news about Tess and the baby.

He heard Sophie before he opened the front door. Those screeches usually meant she'd had it with staying in the playpen while Mommy and Daddy were otherwise occupied. He followed the noise.

The playpen sat in the hall. Sophie had pulled herself up on the side facing one of the guestrooms, where her parents were painting the walls pale blue. Damon was using the roller and Phil was detailing with a brush. While keeping their eyes on their work, they were trying to cajole Sophie into settling down.

She was having none of it. She'd tossed every one of her toys out and stood yelling and rattling the side of the playpen in a bid for attention.

"Hey, Sophie!" Zeke reached the playpen and scooped her up with his good arm. "What's the matter, kid? Don't you approve of that color?"

"Oh, Zeke, thank God." Phil glanced up from where she was kneeling on a piece of foam and pushed her red hair off her forehead with the back of her hand. "What happened to your beard?"

"It got itchy."

"I completely understand." Damon pulled a bandanna from his back pocket and mopped his sweaty face. "That's one reason I don't have a beard, the other being Phil wouldn't like it. Listen, we really want to get the second coat finished before lunch but Sophie has other ideas."

"No problem. I'll watch her for you."

"Great. Her high chair's set up in the kitchen and there's a box of Cheerios on the counter if you want to sprinkle some in her tray. That'll keep her busy for a while."

"Do you care if I take her outside for a little walk around the place?"

Damon laughed. "You can walk her all the way into town if you have the energy."

"But put on her bonnet if you'll be in the sun," Phil said.

"We'll stay in the shade, won't we, sweetheart?" Zeke wasn't taking a chance on burning her fair skin. She was her mother's mini-me when it came to coloring—same red hair and eyes blue as a Wyoming sky. But although she hadn't ended up with Damon's brown eyes, she had his chin. Damon didn't think so but Zeke could definitely see it.

"Thanks, bro," Damon said. "I owe you a beer for this."

"I'll put it on your tab. By the way, have either of you talked to Rosie today?"

"No," Phil said. "Why?"

"Just wondered."

Damon's eyebrows lifted. "Is something going on that we should know about?"

"Yeah, but it can wait until lunch. Come on, Sophie. I'll show you around your famous uncle's ranch."

She bounced in his arms and made a grab for his hat.

"Oh, no, you don't." He left his hat in her playpen and headed down the hall and out the front door. When she pointed to the sparrows hopping around in the tree in the front yard, he walked her over so she could look up through the branches.

She stared at everything as if memorizing it for a test later. She solemnly studied the leaves moving in the breeze, the chattering birds and a caterpillar she spotted on the trunk. Zeke held her close enough to the insect so she could see but not grab it. She'd try to eat it for sure.

Then he walked with her around to the back of the house where they startled a rabbit hiding under a bush. As it scampered away, Sophie crowed with delight and clapped her pudgy hands together. Such a simple thing, a cute little bunny, and she acted as if it was the most amazing experience in the world.

Because she soaked up her environment like a sponge, Zeke got a kick out of showing her things. He crouched so she could get a better look at a beetle pushing its way through the scrub grass. When a hawk soared overhead, he pointed to it and she watched it until it was a tiny speck in the sky.

A downspout was dripping from the brief rain they'd had during the night. He let her catch the drops on her finger and laughed with her as the cool water tickled her skin. That was where they were when Phil came looking for them.

Phil gave him an amused smile. "I almost hate to break this up. You're one heck of a babysitter."

"Beginner's luck. I haven't spent much time with little kids." He handed Sophie over to her mother and they started back toward the front of the house.

"No one would ever know it."

"Maybe it's because I click with Sophie."

"Nah, I don't think that's it. I'll bet you'd be fine no matter whose kid it was." She climbed the porch steps. "Damon's fixing lunch so I hope you're okay with turkey sandwiches."

"Love 'em." He opened the door for her. So she thought he had a talent for taking care of little kids. Interesting.

But playing with Sophie once in a while was a long way from assuming total care for a child. Tess didn't think he was temperamentally suited for it, and she could be right. He couldn't argue with her logic that he was untested and that his lifestyle hadn't prepared him to be a dad. But prepared or not, he *was* a dad, or would be in another six months.

Phil cut up some melon and a banana for Sophie to eat with her fingers. That and the cereal kept her content while the adults ate their sandwiches and chips.

Zeke grabbed a kitchen stool out of a closet and Damon and Phil each took a folding chair. Damon adjusted the old straw hat he liked to wear while he was working and looked across the card table at Zeke. "So, what's up?"

"I got somebody pregnant."

"Get outta town!" Damon's eyes widened. "Didn't we teach you better than that?"

Zeke lowered his voice even though Sophie was too little to understand. "I used condoms, okay? And turns out she had a five percent chance of getting pregnant, so this baby never should have happened, but he did."

Phil put down her sandwich. "Did you say *he*? You already know it's a boy?"

"They have this blood test. Didn't you guys use it?"

Damon shook his head. "No way, no how. There are so few cool surprises anymore that we both decided to wait and see. Anticipation is half the fun." He winced, and Zeke suspected Phil had kicked him under the table. "Not that there's a thing wrong with finding out in advance, if that's what you two decided. It makes the naming thing way easier and you don't get a bunch of yellow baby clothes."

"I wasn't part of the decision." Now Zeke wished he had been because he liked the idea of waiting. "She didn't notify me of this until yesterday and she's already three months along."

"Three months?" Phil eyed him warily. "Um, okay. I'm not sure where to start with the questions. Maybe you'd better just explain in your own words, as they say."

He did his best, but no matter how he prettied up the details, it was still a two-night stand with someone he'd never expected to see again. Now she was the mother of his child.

"So you guys have no history," Damon said. "I mean, apart from the obvious."

"That's right." Zeke took a deep breath and let it out. "I proposed to her this morning and she rejected me."

"What a shocker." Phil shook her head. "Sweetie, no woman worth her salt is going to accept an offer of marriage when it's clear she only got it because of her delicate condition."

Zeke bristled. "There's more to it than that. I like her. A lot."

"Oh, brother of mine, you have so much to learn. Liking her a lot is the equivalent of a friendly handshake. Women don't swoon into your arms because you admit to liking them a lot."

Phil nodded. "He's right, Zeke. I hope you didn't tell her that."

"No, because she never gave me the chance. She said I was crazy and there was no way she was marrying someone she barely knew."

"Ha." Phil smiled. "I like her already. What's her name? I have a feeling we could become friends."

"Tess. Tess Irwin. She teaches first grade over in Casper."

"Sounds like an intelligent woman," Phil said. "Plus she has experience with small children. If you had to get someone pregnant, Tess seems an excellent choice."

"Oh, she's intelligent, all right. She has everything figured out so that I don't have to be involved at all. She's ready to take on the entire responsibility and cut me out of the picture." His voice shook a little. He needed to calm the heck down.

Damon gazed at him for long enough that Zeke squirmed in his chair. Finally, Damon spoke. "The guy I spent all those years with at Thunder Mountain would have been thrilled with that scenario."

"I thought I would be, too, but I'm not. I hate the idea of her taking off with our kid and raising him however she sees fit."

"At least she's spent time with kids," Damon said. "Like Phil said, a teacher seems like a good bet."

"Yeah, on paper she looks great. But what if she screws it up? She knows kids but she's never had one of her own, somebody she has to worry about twenty-four-seven." His stomach churned. "What if…what if she gets tired of being a mother and *takes off*?"

Silence descended over the table except for some little gurgling and cooing noises from Sophie.

Damon glanced at Phil. "Would you please go check Sophie's diaper? She hasn't been changed in a while."

"Sure." Phil unlatched the tray holding Sophie in place and picked her up. "We'll be in the far bedroom if you need us for anything."

"Thanks, hon."

"You bet." She and Sophie left the kitchen.

Damon leaned forward. "Look, I know your mom took off when you were just a little guy, but you know that's not likely to happen."

"Yeah, I know." Zeke had regretted the words the minute they'd left his mouth. But when it came to his unborn son, it was his deepest fear.

"Thunder Mountain guys have a twisted view of what's normal because we didn't get normal. But putting aside your understandable paranoia, do you think this woman is capable of abandoning her child?"

"Probably not." Zeke heaved a sigh. "I'd say the chances are slim to none."

"Then it might be really good if you can trust her to be a good mom. Even better, you could let her know that you have confidence that she'll be a good mom. Wrestling her for control of this baby won't end well."

"You're right, damn it. But I want to be part of my son's life and she sees me as a detriment."

"Then it's up to you to change her mind."

"I know, but how?"

"For starters, have her talk to Phil. When it comes to handling little kids, Phil thinks you're the bomb."

"You know, that's not a bad idea. She's supposed to text me this afternoon so we can talk some more. If you and Phil don't mind sticking around, I could have her come over. Rosie's claimed this baby as her grandson, so that makes him Sophie's cousin."

"And Phil and I are the aunt and uncle." Damon grinned. "Hey, Auntie Phil, are you about done in there?"

"Why, yes, we are," she called as she came from the far end of the house. "But what's this 'Auntie Phil' stuff?"

"Since Rosie assumes every kid fathered by her boys is her grandchild, that makes us officially Aunt Phil and Uncle Damon."

"So it does!" She rubbed noses with Sophie. "What do you think of that, Soph? You'll have a little boy cousin to boss around."

"She'll be the boss of him, all right." Damon chuckled. "Sophie will always be the reigning princess of the cousins. She'll definitely rule over…whatever his name will be. Does he have one yet?"

"I don't think so. But that's another thing I want a say in. What if she decides to name him something dorky? No kid of mine is gonna be saddled with Elmer or Hubert."

"I kind of like Hubert," Damon said. "I was thinking if we had a boy next time, that would be a good… um…" He busted out laughing at Phil's expression of horror. "What? You don't like the name or you're not ready for another kid?"

"Both! In fact, Zeke's sad tale of condom failure is making me nervous. I'm not saying we shouldn't have another one but, dear God, not for two or three years."

"I promise to buy only top-of-the-line condoms from now on."

Phil gasped. "From now on? You don't already?"

"Well…"

"That does it. I'm tossing all the ones we have and you need to go shopping before I have anything to do with you, buddy."

Zeke decided not to mention he'd bought top-of-the-line and made sure the expiration date was a long way off. When his son was old enough to hear the facts about of life, Zeke would explain that having sex with a woman implied that a guy was ready to accept the consequences. But if Tess continued on her current path, that little talk between father and son would never take place.

He picked up his lunch dishes and loaded them into the dishwasher. "I need to run out to the truck and get my phone. I'll invite Tess over here, if that's all right with you guys? I think it would be good for her to meet you."

"Excellent." Phil nodded. "I want to meet her, too."

Damon's eyes shone with approval. "That's a power move, bro. Congratulations."

"How long do you expect to be here?"

"If Sophie takes a nice long nap, we could be around until four," Phil said. "And I think she will. She's been pretty active all morning."

"Good. That should work out perfectly." But when he got to the truck and grabbed his phone from the console, he realized he'd given Tess his number but he didn't have hers. He'd have to call Rosie.

Then he noticed the old brochure peeking out from under the pad of paper Tess had used. He picked the pad up and, sure enough, she would have seen the picture of him with his dad. She hadn't asked him about it, though.

Maybe she didn't want to pry. He hoped that was it because the other possibility was depressing as hell. Maybe she hadn't asked because she didn't want to know more about him. The less she knew, the easier it would be to shut him out of their child's life.

Chapter Six

After lunch, Tess took a notebook out on the front porch so she could jot down some items for her next meeting with Zeke. She didn't know whether he was a reader or not, but if he wanted to be part of this baby's life, he had some homework to do. She started a list of child-care books she had, either physically on her shelf or that she'd downloaded to her phone.

She'd present him with the list and see what happened. Either he'd ignore it, proving to her that he didn't want to bother increasing his knowledge, or he'd read them. Reading them might be enough to discourage him from diving into fatherhood. If it didn't…she'd burn that bridge when she came to it.

She'd come up with nine titles and was trying to remember a tenth when Rosie joined her on the porch. "Zeke's on the phone." She held up her cell. "He said he would have called you but he didn't get your number."

"I guess that's right. Do you mind if I talk to him on your phone?"

"Be my guest. Bring it to me whenever you're finished."

"I won't be long if you want to wait."

"You don't mind my eavesdropping?"

Tess smiled. "Nope." She put the phone to her ear. "Hi, Zeke."

"Hi. I had an idea. Damon and Phil are over here working on the house. They're Sophie's mom and dad."

"I remember."

"We were talking about this cousin thing, and they'd love to meet you. They plan to work until around four, but if you came over about three thirty, they'll knock off early so they have a chance to meet you. Oh, Phil says you'll have to excuse her because she'll be a mess."

"That's okay."

"You could meet little Sophie, too. After they leave, we could go get a bite to eat in town, keep talking."

"I hadn't thought about the fact that the baby already has a cousin."

"He does, and she's a trip."

Although Tess wasn't sure Zeke was the right father figure for her son, she loved the idea that his foster family was eager to welcome the baby into the fold. Her traditional parents might very well disown her, so Thunder Mountain Ranch might be her only port in a storm. "I'll be over at three thirty." With her list.

"Great. Rosie can give you directions. See you then."

"'Bye." She ended the call and handed the phone back to Rosie, who'd taken the Adirondack chair next to hers. "I'm driving over so I can meet Sophie and her folks."

"That's marvelous. You'll love them. They're both construction geniuses and they're doing so well with their company these days. Always in demand, especially for renovations. Matt's place is a labor of love, though. I'm sure they're not charging him what they should."

"And where is he? Why is Zeke watching the place? I was never clear on that."

"He's on location filming another Western, this time in Calgary."

"He's a filmmaker?"

"No, he's the star. Maybe I never mentioned it—he's Matt Forrest."

Tess blinked. "Matt Forrest, the actor? The one who was on the cover of all the tabloids last month?"

"One and the same. Fortunately the video he made publicizing the academy caused people to forget about that bogus scandal. I thought everybody in the world had seen it by now and knew that he was a member of the Thunder Mountain Brotherhood."

"You know, that must have come out at the same time I found out I was pregnant. I spent a couple of weeks holed up in my house trying to figure out what the heck to do. I didn't watch the news or go online."

"Doesn't matter. But that's why Zeke's over there watching the place, at least until he goes back on the rodeo circuit. Sometime before then we'll figure out a more permanent solution. The bigger Matt gets, the more he'll need that ranch as a getaway."

Tess gazed at Rosie. "Matt Forrest is going to be my baby's uncle."

"Now you're getting the idea. That little guy will

have more awesome aunts, uncles and cousins than you can shake a stick at. Isn't that great?"

"Yes, Rosie. It sure is."

Two hours later Tess parked next to Zeke's truck in the driveway of a single-story ranch house painted mustard yellow. The paint didn't look fresh, so she'd bet Damon and Phil would be changing it. It wasn't hard to recognize their truck with its extension ladders, tarps and large paint buckets in the back, along with a roomy storage locker tucked up against the rear window.

Knowing she'd be interacting with a seven-month-old, she'd put her hair in a ponytail and changed her hoop earrings to posts. Maybe the little girl wouldn't want to be held, but if she did, Tess was prepared. She left her purse and her list of books in the car.

When she walked around to the front of the house, she found Zeke on the porch steps playing peekaboo with Sophie, who was every bit as cute as Rosie had said.

Zeke looked up and smiled.

Oh, no. That tug at her heart couldn't be happening. To lust after this big cowboy was one thing, but the feeling swamping her now was a thousand times more tender and intimate. She didn't want anything to do with it.

Sophie took advantage of Zeke's momentary distraction to pop up for a second and knock his hat off. Then she laughed.

"Hey, Sophie. We talked about that." He retrieved the hat and laid it brim-side up on the steps. Carefully balancing the baby in his arms, he stood. "Uncle Zeke's hat is special. He put it on so he could look good for your aunt Tess."

Sophie gazed up at him, her expression innocent. Then she bounced in his arms and grabbed his nose. More baby laughter.

Zeke was obviously trying hard not to laugh with her. "The nose is special, too." He glanced over at Tess. "She was excited about meeting you so I brought her out here to wait." He turned so the little girl was facing her. "Sophie, this is your aunt Tess, the one I've been telling you about. She's going to have a baby boy who'll be your cousin. He doesn't have a name yet—at least, I don't think he does."

"He doesn't."

"Good." He kept his attention on Sophie.

"Mmm." She made eye contact with the baby. "Hello, Sophie. Your uncle Zeke says you're a trip. Is that right?"

Sophie gave her the once-over. Apparently, Tess passed muster, because the little girl held out both arms and gave a little wiggle that clearly said she was ready to trade partners.

"See what a good sales job I did?" Zeke came closer, bringing with him the citrus scent of his aftershave. He handed Sophie to her.

The aroma reminded her of this morning on Lion's Rest Rock when he'd proposed. That awkward moment stood in stark contrast to this one, which was filled with warm emotions and a cuddly baby girl. Then she realized he must have reapplied the aftershave because it wouldn't have lasted this many hours. Now that she was paying better attention, she could tell that he'd shaved again, too.

No question he was attempting to get on her good side. He was doing an excellent job of it, too. But decisions she made now would affect her baby for a lifetime. She'd be very careful not to make the wrong ones.

"I hear the Shop-Vac," Zeke said, "so Damon and Phil must be cleaning up the work area. Sophie has a well-baby checkup at four fifteen but the doctor's office isn't that far so they can hang out here for a while."

"I admire them for taking her on the job with them." Tess enjoyed carrying the baby as they climbed the steps and crossed the porch. A few months ago she would have battled feelings of jealousy, but no more.

"Damon said they might not be able to bring her for much longer." Zeke opened the door for her. "She doesn't sleep as much and she's not as happy in her playpen now that she can crawl. They're looking at options, at least part-time."

"Because you won't be around later on."

"Right."

And the same would be true for the baby she was carrying. Once he got back to his roping career, chances were good he'd lose interest. While he was recuperating he had time on his hands, time to play with Sophie and imagine that he'd be thrilled with fatherhood. If she let nature take its course, he'd eventually realize his lifestyle didn't leave room for children.

But that wasn't her personality. She preferred a definite plan so she'd know exactly what to expect from him. Taking a wait-and-see attitude would drive her nuts. That was where the reading list would come in. It was his first hurdle.

Damon was vacuuming up sawdust when they

walked in. He gave the floor one last swipe and switched the Shop-Vac off before walking over to Tess. "Pleased to meet you. I'm Damon." His smile encompassed both her and his daughter. "I see you and Sophie are already acquainted."

"Da-da!" Sophie squirmed and reached for her father.

Damon's gaze softened. "Hey, Soph." He lifted her into his arms. "Who's your daddy?"

"Da-da!" She patted his cheeks with both hands.

"I think she finally gets that da-da is me." Damon looked besotted. "Knocks me out every time she says it."

Zeke laughed. "She's working you, bro. Laying the groundwork. Won't be long before she'll be asking da-da for a pony."

"And he'll get her one, too." A tall redhead walked into the living room carrying a collapsed playpen. "Good thing the property is zoned for it or we'd have to move." She leaned the playpen against the wall and came over, hand outstretched. "Hi, I'm Phil."

Tess wasn't surprised that Phil had a firm grip. She seemed to be a very self-possessed woman. "Your daughter is adorable."

"Most of the time." Phil's expression was warm and friendly. "But you're a teacher. You know the frustrations that crop up with kids."

"I do, but you're lucky that she's so social. That's a big plus."

"Comes with the territory around here. She's been passed from one adoring person to another ever since she was born."

"Nice." Tess had taught kids like that. They were

easier to deal with because they'd learned early that the world was a benevolent and welcoming place. If the Thunder Mountain guys hadn't experienced that advantage, they might be more eager to provide it for the next generation.

Phil glanced around the bare living room. "I'd invite you to sit down but we only have a couple of folding chairs. Oh, and the queen bed in the master bedroom."

Tess didn't want to think about where Zeke was sleeping, thank you very much. "I'm fine with sitting on the floor."

"Hey," Zeke said. "Let's do what we did over at Thunder Mountain a couple of weeks ago and make a circle that Sophie can crawl around in."

"Oh, yeah," Damon said. "She'd love that."

As they formed a loose circle and Damon sat the little girl in the middle, Tess couldn't help thinking of how much fun it would be to have her baby fussed over like this. She might make a trip to Sheridan a couple of times a month. Even then, he wouldn't bond with everyone the way Sophie had. These were the trade-offs she'd have to make and the decisions weren't easy ones.

Zeke sat on the opposite side of the circle from Tess, which gave her a great view of his expression as he coaxed Sophie over to sit in his lap. He was into it. She reminded herself that he probably welcomed the distraction since he wasn't roping these days. Still, watching him interact with the baby tugged on her heart yet again.

Sophie made a game out of musical laps and obviously loved being the center of attention. Meanwhile Phil managed to work some adult conversation into the mix. First she asked Tess how long she'd be staying this time.

Tess didn't miss Phil's "this time" reference, but that was okay. She'd already decided to accept Rosie and Herb's warm hospitality on a regular basis. "I'll probably go home in the next day or two," she said. "But this morning Lexi invited me to the wedding, so I'll be back in September."

"Hey, that's great!" Phil looked genuinely pleased.

Judging from Zeke's expression, he hadn't been expecting that, but he didn't seem upset about it.

"If you'll be coming back in a few weeks," Phil said, "I can pack up some of Sophie's newborn outfits if you want them. Since we didn't announce whether we were having a boy or girl, they're unisex, but you should know there's a lot of yellow, in case you're not fond of that color."

"Yellow's very cheerful and I guarantee the baby won't care what color he's wearing. Thank you. That would be wonderful."

"Rosie will want to get you some things, I'm sure. Knowing her, she'll find a onesie that looks like he's wearing jeans and a Western shirt." Phil reached into her pocket for a tissue and wiped some drool from Sophie's face before the little girl motored toward Tess. "Rosie must be so excited that there's another Thunder Mountain baby on the way."

"She is. Everybody's been great." Sophie climbed onto Tess's lap, grabbing handfuls of her shirt as she pulled herself upright. "Well, hello, there, sweetie. Look who's standing up. Such a big girl."

Sophie chortled with pride, swayed a little and sat again with a thump.

"Once she starts walking," Damon said, "life as we know it will be over."

"That'll be fun to see," Zeke said. "How soon do you figure?"

Damon glanced over at Zeke. "Not soon enough for you, I'm afraid. I'm thinking another two months at least, maybe three. But you'll be outta here by then, right?"

"Guess so."

"We'll send video," Phil said. "We have Drew Martinelli on standby."

"I met her today." The longer they chatted, the more Tess felt part of the group. "She came over to talk about the wedding venue."

Phil perked up. "Was anything decided?"

"I think so. But I don't know if I'm supposed to say anything."

"Yeah, go ahead." Damon settled Sophie in his lap. "Secrets don't last long around here, and I'll bet this isn't even a secret. We've heard rumors. Is it the barn?"

"Yep." But Tess wouldn't give any more details. Damon or Cade should talk to Zeke about becoming an official member of the brotherhood. Then they could discuss the plan to arrange the brotherhood in a semi-circle behind the bride and groom.

"I knew it." Phil said. "That makes perfect sense for Cade and Lexi. They've worked together in that barn since they were teenagers."

"I didn't realize that." Tess envied them their long relationship. They'd had plenty of time to make sure they belonged together.

Phil glanced at her phone. "Well, folks, we need to

get moving. We—" A distant clap of thunder interrupted whatever she'd been about to say.

Sophie squealed and buried her face against her father's shoulder.

"It's okay, Soph." Damon stroked her back. "Just some old guys up in the clouds bowling."

"But if it's going to rain soon, that's all the more reason to head out." Phil stood and walked over to the folded playpen. "If it comes down fast, that dirt road can turn to mud in no time."

"Maybe I should go, too." Tess got to her feet. She could easily picture the dirt road she'd driven in on turning into a slippery mess. "My car doesn't have four-wheel drive."

"Shouldn't be a problem." Zeke came to stand beside her.

"In case I do end up leaving, though, I need to bring in something from my car." She wasn't going to take off without presenting him with her reading list.

He nodded. "Fair enough. We'll go get that and decide whether the storm's going to be a problem. Sometimes there's a lot of noise and then it just hangs over the mountains. Here, Phil, let me carry the playpen out to the truck."

"Thanks, Zeke. And thanks for saving the day earlier. Without you there to entertain Sophie, we wouldn't have made such good progress."

"It was fun. She's a great kid."

Tess began to wonder if she'd been invited over primarily to observe Zeke with Sophie. It was a logical move. He'd been clear enough that he wanted to be part of his baby's life. Damon and Phil would want to help in any way they could. She had a hunch he'd told them about his proposal—and her refusal.

If they were holding that against her, they'd disguised it well. More likely they were of the same opinion as Rosie, that a proposal wasn't appropriate at this stage and might never be. They were delighted about the baby, though.

Tess had never dreamed that a trip to Sheridan would bring her into contact with so many people who were excited about the pregnancy. No matter how things turned out with Zeke, she'd always be grateful for his foster family.

Chapter Seven

Zeke was happy about the way the visit with Phil, Damon and Sophie had gone. He could tell it had put Tess in a mellow mood and he wanted to build on that. After Damon piled his little family into the work truck and they drove away, Zeke glanced up at the thunderclouds nestled against the mountains. "Doesn't look too bad."

Tess opened her car door. "Tell you what. We'll sit on the porch while I show you what I brought. Then I should probably head back. I don't want to get stuck here."

He wished she hadn't said it as though it were a bad thing. He'd always enjoyed the cozy feeling of being with someone he liked while a storm raged outside. Obviously she wasn't looking at it that way.

His original plan, to drive into town for a bite to eat,

didn't seem as appealing with a storm coming. Phil was right about the dirt road turning treacherous in no time. Grading and paving it, or at least laying down a bed of gravel, was on Matt's list, but the project was on hold until he decided what he wanted.

Zeke had half a mind to rent a grader and do a basic job himself. Now that Tess could be driving back and forth on it, he just might. If he could get hold of a grader first thing in the morning, he'd be finished by noon. Then he could invite her over for a candle-light dinner. Just dinner. No funny business unless she wanted to. He'd promised her she was in charge on that score.

Unfortunately he'd also been a jerk about how he'd said it. The hike up to Lion's Rest had been a disaster from start to finish. The proposal had been a huge mistake and, on top of that, he'd brought up his legal rights. That couldn't have endeared him to her.

This afternoon he'd talked with Damon and Phil about the situation. They weren't absolutely sure, but they thought his case might be weak if Tess challenged him in court. He had specifically told her that he never wanted kids. And since he couldn't lie under oath, he was permanently branded with that statement.

Tess grabbed her purse out of the car. "I just real-ized you don't have chairs on the front porch. I was thinking of Thunder Mountain."

"I'll bring the folding chairs out of the kitchen," he said as they walked around to the front of the house. "I don't know about you, but I like sitting on the porch and watching the clouds."

"I like that, too." She started up the steps. "I'll help you get them."

"Thanks, but I'll handle it."

"Zeke, you have an injured shoulder and I can carry a folding chair."

"I'm sure you can, but it would be my pleasure to bring it to you." He held her gaze. "Would you let me do that?" He watched the wary look in her eyes change to something else, something that made his heart pound and his groin ache.

Abruptly she turned away. "Thank you."

"You're welcome." He shook with desire as he walked into the house. Damn, that woman was potent. In the kitchen he braced both hands against the counter and sucked in air. The pain in his shoulder reminded him that putting his weight on his left arm wasn't a great idea.

Pushing away from the counter, he swore softly. If the condom hadn't been faulty—but, no, he couldn't wish things had been different. She was overjoyed to be pregnant. Now that he'd had time to think about it, he was glad she was, too. He wouldn't have chosen to have a kid, but when something this unlikely happened, maybe it was meant to be.

He should get back out there before she came searching for him. He barely trusted himself to be alone with her on the porch, but if she came inside and her blue eyes held the same kind of promise, then…he'd resist her unless she straight-out asked him to take the next step.

Folding each chair with a snap, he carried them with his good arm through the living room and out to the front porch. She was leaning against the railing with her back to him. He paused, noticing how her ponytail had exposed the tender skin at her nape.

If they were still lovers, he'd put down the chairs, walk over and wrap his arms around her waist. Then he'd nuzzle that vulnerable spot, one he happened to know was an erogenous zone for her. He'd learned a fair bit about her body in that Texas hotel room. Not so much about her, though, which was telling.

But then she hadn't learned much about him, either. They'd both preferred it that way. Sex with a semi-stranger had been a new experience for her, but was his typical way of operating.

She turned. No doubt she'd heard him come through the door. "The clouds are moving away. The storm may not be a problem."

"Then we could drive into town for dinner like we planned."

"I don't think we need to trouble ourselves. Let me show you my list and then I'll go back to Thunder Mountain."

"Your list of what?" He set up the chairs, mindful of putting a respectful distance between them.

"Books." She handed him a sheet of paper and took a seat.

He sat and scanned the paper. "I take it you want me to read these?"

"You're adamant that you want to step into the role of our baby's dad, so, yes, I do."

He glanced at her. "I like that you said *our baby*. That might be the first time you've done that."

"Oh, I doubt it. Obviously we were both involved, so I'm pretty sure I've acknowledged—"

"I'm pretty sure you haven't."

She waved a hand in the air. "Whatever."

"No, not *whatever*. This is important, Tess. This

morning you told me to think of myself as a sperm donor." The phrase still curdled his blood.

She faced him, regret in her blue eyes. "That was a terrible thing to say and I'm sorry."

"It was terrible, but my angry reaction told me something about myself. I might not have planned for this to happen, but now that it has, I reject the idea of being a sperm donor. I'm this baby's father. I admit the reality hasn't fully registered, but give me time. I intend to get there."

"Then you need to read these books."

"I will. I'll see how many are available in town and I'll order the rest." He tapped the paper. "You put time into this. I appreciate it."

"You do? You don't think it's arrogant of me to hand you a recommended reading list?"

"Are you kidding? Reading is a great way to learn a skill. My dad had a bunch of books on—well, never mind. It's beside the point." Oh, man, he hadn't meant to get into his past.

"I saw the brochure."

He sighed. "I figured you had."

"So you and your dad were a team?"

"Yep." What a mess. He didn't want to talk about his dad, but at least she'd asked. In the space of a few minutes she'd referred to "our baby," apologized for calling him a sperm donor and showed interest in his father. "Rosie didn't fill you in?"

"She said it wasn't her information to provide."

He should have known. Rosie had told her boys the tale belonged to the protagonist. He'd looked up that word after she'd used it and had figured out the protagonist of his tale was him.

"We were a team." He figured he might as well tell her all of it and get it over with. "My mom left when I was pretty small. I don't remember her. My dad tried to be there for me. He did the best he could, but I realize now he must have been depressed." He looked at her. "That can be genetic."

"I know. I'm glad you told me, but I'll think positive that the baby won't inherit the predisposition for it. You didn't."

"How can you tell? Like you said, we barely know each other."

"That's true, but if you were clinically depressed, Rosie would have said so. She's trained in spotting the signs, too. She wasn't ready to tell me your life story but she wouldn't have left me out of the loop on something that critical."

"You're right. And it would have come up in my counseling sessions."

"You had counseling?"

"It's practically a given when your dad commits suicide."

Her face drained of color. "Oh, no." She put her hand on his arm. "How old were you?"

"Fourteen."

"Fourteen." She swallowed. "I can't... Dear God, that must have been horrible."

He nodded. Her sympathetic reaction stirred up feelings of sadness he'd thought were long gone. Then again, he didn't have reason to tell the story anymore. Rosie and Herb had known before they'd brought him to Thunder Mountain.

He'd told the other guys living at the ranch because they'd asked with the straightforward curiosity of those who had also been through hell. Then he'd tucked the story away. He hadn't shared it with anyone on the circuit or any of the women he'd dated. No point in it.

Tess gave his arm a little squeeze and moved her hand away.

He wished she'd left it there. He missed her touch. Sure, they'd gotten together for sex, but she communicated warmth with her touch and the pleasure of human contact. Maybe that was why he hadn't dated anyone since that weekend in April. She'd been special and he'd wanted to savor the memories for a while.

She took a deep breath and let it out. "Is that why you didn't want to get married and have children? You were afraid your father's depression would be passed on?"

"My dad always said you couldn't count on anybody and in the end I couldn't even count on him. I haven't wanted anyone depending on me, either."

"How's that worked out for you?"

"Great."

"See? Getting involved with this baby would be a huge mistake. Obviously my life will change and I look forward to it. Yours doesn't have to."

"It already has, Tess. This afternoon I was mentally rehearsing what I'd say when he's ready for *the talk*."

"You're kidding, right? Although I can see why that topic would be on your mind."

"I'm not kidding."

"Huh." She seemed taken aback. "Then I'm way behind you. I'm still researching when to introduce peanut butter."

"You mean so he has less chance of developing an allergy?"

"How did you know?"

"Phil and Damon. They talk about baby stuff all the time. Until now, I didn't pay much attention. Now I will." He also made a mental note that a woman who'd research whether to give a baby peanut butter wasn't likely to walk off and leave the kid.

He should dial back the paranoia, like Damon had said. He should, but he hadn't. He needed to spend more time with her before he'd be convinced. Folding her recommended reading list in fourths, he tucked it in the front pocket of his jeans. "It's possible Phil and Damon have some of these they could loan me, but whether they do or not, I'll get them read."

"Okay."

Something about the way she said it alerted him to the truth. The books were a test—one she didn't expect him to pass. She figured he'd never make it through her long list. She *wanted* him to fail at this father thing.

That stuck in his craw. "You know what? There's still time for me to drive into town and see what books I can pick up. Were you serious about heading home? Because that's fine with—" A low growl of thunder grabbed his attention as rain began to patter on the roof. For the first time since they'd sat on the porch, he noticed his surroundings.

Sheets of rain obscured the mountains and a rising wind swept the downpour onto the porch. Damn it. He'd been so involved in the conversation he'd lost track of the weather.

She picked up her purse and stood. "I'll make a run for it."

"No."

"It just started. If I leave right now I'll be fine."

"I don't trust that road. It gets bad fast."

"Then I need to hurry." She started toward the steps.

"Tess, no." He caught her arm and pulled her back. "My truck would probably make it, but if I drive you to Thunder Mountain your car will still be here, which will be a nuisance for you. Let's just wait it out." He decided to maintain his hold on her arm until he'd convinced her not to leave the shelter of the porch.

She looked from him to the heavy curtains of rain.

"Take my word for it." He held her gaze. "The chances are very good that you'll get stuck in the mud out there. Then I'll have to come and pull you out, which wouldn't be a whole lot of fun for either of us."

Her shoulders relaxed and she let out a breath. "You're right. It's just that I got the distinct impression you wanted me to leave."

"I did until it started raining in biblical proportions."

She glanced down at his hand on her arm. "Well, I promise not to take off, so you can let go of me."

He released her. "It might be a quick storm. If the sun comes out right after, the road will dry in no time." The steady pounding on the roof didn't sound like the rain was about to let up, but anything was possible.

"May I ask why you're so eager to get rid of me all of a sudden?"

"Sure." He pulled the list out of his pocket and waved it in front of her. "Do you really want me to read all these?"

"Of course. Why else would I make up the list?"

"To give me a job you don't expect me to finish. There's a chance I'm not into reading. Some guys, maybe even a lot of guys, aren't. So if I don't complete this list, you can say I'm not dedicated enough to being a father to our kid." He'd guessed right. He could see it in the pink flush of her cheeks and her uneasy glance.

She cleared her throat and lifted her chin. "Raising a child takes knowledge, hard work and dedication."

So prim and proper. Motherhood had given her a glow he found irresistible, but it had made her a tad self-righteous. He recalled the generous nature of the woman he'd known in April and wondered if that woman was still in there. "You've seen me perform in the arena. How do you suppose I reached that level of expertise?"

"Point taken, but you love to rope. I have serious doubts that you'll love being a father. If you can't make it through these books, then it's possible being a parent isn't your thing."

He could tell she was hoping he'd bomb out because she wanted the job all to herself. She could guarantee parenting would be done the way she wanted it. They were so alike that it almost made him smile, except he was still irritated with her. "It's also possible that the books are dry as dust, or that I learn better through doing something other than reading. As a teacher, I'm sure you understand there are different styles of learning."

"I do." She squared her shoulders.

"That said, I intend to finish every title you suggested. Now let's go inside and make some coffee. It's cold and wet out here." He walked to the door, opened it and touched the tips of his fingers to the brim of his hat. "After you, ma'am."

Chapter Eight

They'd no sooner walked into Matt's house than Rosie called Zeke's cell phone. Tess watched his face light up as he talked to her. "Yes, ma'am, she's still here. No, ma'am, I won't let her drive back unless it's safe." He listened some more. "I do, as a matter of fact. Can you describe again how you make it?"

Tess figured out he was getting some cooking instructions. Dinnertime wasn't far away and, sure enough, her stomach was reminding her of it. But Zeke didn't have to cook for her. Maybe he had some snacks that would take the edge off her hunger until she could drive back to Thunder Mountain. She walked over and tapped him on the shoulder.

"Just a sec," he told his foster mom. "Tess is trying to get my attention." He turned to her. "What's up?"

"You don't need to fix me dinner."

"Because you're going to fix me dinner instead?" There was a twinkle in his eyes.

"Well, I hadn't—"

"We both need to eat and I'm pretty sure I have all the ingredients for Rosie's meat loaf. Let me get the details and we can make it together."

This was sounding much cozier than she'd intended but she was suddenly starving. She might ask about snacks, after all, because the meat loaf would take a while. "I'll grab the chairs from the porch."

"Just leave them. I'll bring them in later."

She ignored him and went to fetch the chairs. She didn't feel like standing around doing nothing, especially because he looked so darned appealing talking to his foster mom. She didn't want to be charmed.

Telling Zeke about her pregnancy had seemed noble and relatively simple until she'd actually done it. Once or twice since coming here she'd wished she'd kept her mouth shut. But then she wouldn't have met his foster family.

As she set the chairs up at the card table in the kitchen, she compared the Zeke Rafferty who'd occupied her thoughts for months with the one she was coming to know now. Making love to someone so unfettered had been liberating, but it hadn't inspired her to change her life.

Afterward she'd returned to the house that she'd been awarded in the divorce. She'd continued teaching small children at a private school. In June she'd spent her obligatory two weeks with her parents in Laramie.

This pregnancy had revived her dream of having a family, but she'd pictured it as a family of two. She'd never imagined sharing this baby with a footloose cowboy who performed rope tricks on the rodeo circuit and likely owned nothing but his truck, his roping equipment and his wardrobe. She'd assumed that he wouldn't want anything to do with parenting. Given the carefree lifestyle he cherished, it made no sense that he'd reverse direction and dig in his heels.

But he had. She wondered if it had anything to do with his foster family. Ordinarily he'd be traveling on the circuit and having minimal contact with them. But he'd been injured. Without that setback, would he be the caretaker of his foster brother's ranch, the babysitter for another foster brother's daughter and a guy eager to make meat loaf?

Although she might be seeing a different Zeke Rafferty now, the one she'd first met could appear the minute his shoulder was healed. He firmly believed that he'd changed because of the imminent birth of his son and she didn't buy it.

How could she possibly challenge his conclusion, though, when his behavior with Sophie and his offer to fix dinner made him seem so domestic? Even worse, if she wanted to be part of this foster family, both for her benefit and that of her son, she should remember that Zeke was a part of it, too. And they were fiercely loyal to each other.

He began wrapping up his phone call. "Yes, ma'am, three-fifty for an hour. Thanks. And if the weather stays nasty, I'll bring Tess home in my truck. We can always work out the logistics of retrieving her car. Right. Have a great evening." He ended the call and turned to her. "Rosie says that if you haven't eaten since lunch, you're probably starving because pregnant ladies are hungry all the time. Are you starving?"

"I'm pretty hungry."

"Then we'll make some snacks before we start on the meat loaf." He put his phone on the counter and opened the refrigerator. "Do you like cheddar cheese?"

"Adore it."

"Me, too." He took a package out of the refrigerator door and reached for the cutting board leaning against the backsplash. "There's a box of crackers in the cupboard by the stove. Oh, and I have a jar of black olives." He opened the refrigerator again and took them out. "Want some?"

"You bet. Hand them over."

He gave her the jar. "If you want a bowl to put them in, dishes are in the top cupboard, far right."

"Got it." She put the olives in a bowl and carried it to the table along with the crackers. She held up the box. "Mind if I go ahead and open these?"

"By all means." He finished slicing the cheese and put the cutting board next to her on the table. "Start eating. I'm going to open a beer, but I know you can't have that. I have some root beer, though."

"Sounds great."

He came back with two bottles and twisted the cap from hers before giving it to her. "Wind's whipping up pretty good out there."

"Guess it is." She's been so intent on their snack that she hadn't paid attention, but now she could hear it gusting through the trees surrounding the house.

"Could be a good sign. Sometimes a strong wind will blow the storm somewhere else." He sat across from her and when he stretched out his long legs, they bumped hers. "Sorry."

"No worries. It's a small table." She tried to keep

from nudging his denim-covered legs but finally gave up the effort. After all, it wasn't as if they'd never been in close proximity. They'd spent hours with their legs tangled together.

"Matt's ordered a table and chairs." He twisted the cap on his beer and took a sip. "But he doesn't want to buy a lot of furniture while Damon and Phil are still working. It'll only get in the way."

"Understandable." She reached for more cheese and crackers. "Excellent snacks, by the way. Thank you."

"You're welcome. I'm glad Rosie clued me in. Would you have said anything?"

"Probably. Being pregnant has made me more assertive about asking for what I want."

"That's good." He tossed an olive in the air and caught it in his mouth.

She'd forgotten that she'd seen him do something similar before. "I guess you don't limit yourself to popcorn for that stunt."

"Nope. It fosters hand-eye coordination, and I need all the extra practice I can get these days." He winked at her. "It also impresses the ladies."

"Trust me, it wasn't the popcorn trick that reeled me in."

"Then what did?"

"I'm not telling." She built herself a double-decker mini sandwich of crackers and cheese and managed to eat it without making a huge mess.

"One thing I remember about you from April is that you didn't eat a lot. That old saying about eating for two must be right."

"Now it is. For the first two and a half months I had no appetite and was often sick to my stomach."

His hazel eyes filled with concern. "That sounds awful."

"If I'd figured out I was pregnant, it wouldn't have been so bad. Morning sickness is common in the first few months. But I knew I couldn't be pregnant. I tried so hard to conceive when I was married and nothing ever worked, so I couldn't imagine that a couple of nights with you—using condoms, no less—would succeed when so many methods had failed."

"I'm still in awe of that. I'd love to claim that it's all because of my superior swimmers, but I think it could just as easily be the phases of the moon."

"Or the phases of my cycle. I went back and checked and that would have been my most fertile time."

"You keep track?" He took a swallow of his beer.

"It's an old habit I can't seem to break. When I was married we both kept track. Jared was determined to have kids."

"Huh."

"You probably can't imagine that." She popped another olive in her mouth. She was tempted to try his trick but decided it was more important to get that thing into her than to play games. The hunger pangs were gradually receding.

He leaned back in his chair and tipped his hat away from his forehead. "You're right. I can't imagine being *determined* to have kids. I realize some couples really want them, but your ex sounds a bit obsessed with the idea."

"I guess he was. When we got tested and found out I had little chance of getting pregnant, I suggested adoption. He wouldn't hear of it. My gynecologist had mentioned an experimental and somewhat risky surgery that might fix the problem. Jared wanted me to do it. When I refused, he filed for divorce."

"That sucks."

"It did at the time." She used to think her life was over and she'd wept buckets, but this baby made up for everything. "In the end he did me a favor."

"And me."

She glanced at him in surprise. "How can you say that? If this hadn't happened, you could have continued living the way you'd always planned. In fact, I've been trying to convince you that's still possible."

"And I've been trying to convince you it's not." The card table was small and when he leaned across it he was very close. "When you told me that you were pregnant with our son, I spent the rest of the night thinking. I asked myself if I regretted being with you in Texas considering the outcome. Well, I don't." His gaze darkened. "You were incredible, Tess. Warm, responsive...lovely."

She should break eye contact. That look, that simmering intensity, had been her kryptonite back in April. Still was now. Her heart pounded as a different kind of hunger, one that had nothing to do with food, begged for satisfaction.

His soft voice wove a seductive spell as he gently stroked her arm. "I don't regret that we made a baby, either. But I think you have regrets."

"No." Her vocal cords felt tight. "I want this child."

"I know you want him. But you don't want me."

Crazy laughter threatened to bubble up. She'd never wanted any man more than she wanted Zeke at this very moment.

He covered her hand with his and held her gaze.

"But be forewarned. I'm not going anywhere." Then he gave her hand a squeeze and pushed away from the table. "Time to make meat loaf."

She took a steadying breath. She'd almost expected him to invite her into his bedroom. God help her, she would have gone, and that would have sent a terrible message. She couldn't agree to sex and yet refuse his help with parenting their son.

While he got out a bowl to mix in the ingredients and a pan for the meat loaf, she closed up the box of crackers and carried the cutting board and the empty olive bowl over to the sink.

"Something almost happened just now." He crumbled hamburger into the bowl.

"It did?"

"You know it did." He kept his gaze on the bowl as he shredded two slices of bread into it.

"I suppose so." She watched him tear up the bread. He had great hands and long, nimble fingers. Those hands could work magic with a rope and they could work magic on a woman's body.

"I said you'd be in charge of it."

"I know."

"I almost didn't let you have the decision. I was seconds away from making a move."

"Why didn't you?"

"A couple of reasons." He glanced over at her. "Does slicing onions bother you?"

"No."

He tilted his head toward the one sitting on the counter. "If you'd chop, I'd be much obliged. Knives are in the—"

"Knife block. I see it." She rinsed off the onion and the cutting board. "What reasons?"

"First off, would sex hurt the baby?"

A flush of desire made her lady parts tingle. "Not unless it's of the 'swinging from the chandeliers' variety." She started cutting up the onion.

He chuckled softly. "We had that kind a time or two."

"I remember." She sniffed.

"Are you crying?"

"Nope. Just a slight reaction to the onion. I'm fine."

"Want me to take over?"

"Absolutely not. I've got this."

"If you're sure. Your eyes are watering."

"Potent onion." She sniffed again and laughed. "Really. I'm not getting emotional." She finished chopping the onion.

He washed his hands and pulled a bandanna out of his back pocket. "Let me wipe your eyes. You have tears running down your cheeks."

"I know, but I promise you I'm not crying." She put down the knife and lifted her face.

"I believe you. I can tell the difference. Hold still." He leaned in and carefully wiped away the tears. "So I have to ask. Did you research the subject of pregnant ladies having sex?" He dabbed at her eyes with the bandanna. "Because if you did, I can't help but be curious as to why."

"Obviously because I'm planning to take a lover."

He sucked in a breath. "Please tell me that's a joke."

"It's a joke. Although you and I have no commitment to each other, so if I wanted to, then—"

"Let it be me." He took her by the shoulders. "Please,

Tess. I know I have no claim, but the thought of you with some other guy makes me crazy."

She looked up at him. "That's a very strange statement for you to make."

"Why?"

"Judging from how you described your love life when we were in Texas, you have a new girlfriend in every town. Yet you expect—"

"Whoa, whoa. Where did you get the idea I have a new girlfriend in every town?"

"You said you never wanted to be tied down and you're a highly sexed man. So, logically that adds up to lots of casual encounters with different women in different parts of the country."

He smiled. "That would make me quite the Romeo, wouldn't it?"

"Aren't you?"

"'Fraid not, ma'am. When you and I got together, I hadn't enjoyed that particular activity in at least six months. Let me think. No, it was seven. And there's been no one since our little episode."

"Why not?"

"Let's just say that I wanted a little longer to savor my memories."

"That's very sweet." Her image of him changed yet again. "I guess I just assumed, because you're so good at it, that you've had a lot of practice."

His smile widened. "It's like riding a bike."

"With some guys, yes. With you it's more like painting a picture or singing a song."

His gaze held hers. "I don't know how you can say a thing like that and not expect me to kiss you."

Her pulse rate shot up. Once he kissed her, the game would be over. They'd never stop with a kiss.

"But I won't kiss you, much as I'd love to." He let go of her and backed away. "I didn't tell you the other reason we're not in the bedroom right now."

She swallowed. "Which is?"

"You might think I seduced you just so I could get what I want."

"Meaning sex?"

He shook his head. "The chance to be our baby's dad."

Chapter Nine

Zeke had surprised himself with his level of self-control, but then again, a lot was at stake. Ever since Tess had arrived, he'd longed to touch her, hold her, even place his hand over the gentle swell of her belly. If he had a loving relationship with her, he'd be allowed to.

If someone had asked him months ago whether he'd have these sentimental feelings, he would've laughed. *Not this cowboy*, he would have said with a cocky smile. And he would have been dead wrong.

He and Tess worked in silence finishing up the meal preparations. He'd remembered to turn on the oven in advance, which was a miracle, all things considered. They put two potatoes in to bake along with the meat loaf and he had the makings for a salad when the meat loaf was nearly ready.

The storm continued to rage outside, which seemed appropriate considering the battle he was having with himself. He'd never spent this much time with a woman he wanted without making some kind of physical overture. Stroking her arm, squeezing her hand and drying her onion tears didn't really count, at least not for much.

He'd had one chance to kiss her and he hadn't taken it. She wouldn't have stopped him. He'd bet his truck on that one.

Yet he wasn't willing to sacrifice his chance to be a father by taking her to bed. Maybe doing that would make things better between them, but it could also make them worse. Back in April they'd enjoyed each other without thinking of the future. Now they wouldn't be able to think about anything else.

Once their meal was in the oven, she walked to the kitchen window and stood, arms wrapped protectively around her middle, as she gazed out at the storm. If they were in a different emotional place, he could move in behind her and guide her back against his chest. They could watch the rain together.

He'd never expected to want that kind of closeness with anyone. But living near Thunder Mountain had thrown him together with several loving couples and he'd had to grudgingly admit he envied them a little.

As it was, he wasn't sure what to do while they waited for dinner to cook. "Sorry there's nowhere else to sit. I don't notice it so much when I'm the only one here."

"That's okay." She turned to him. "I keep forgetting this is a movie star's house."

"Doesn't look much like it with no furniture, sawhorses sitting around and tarps rolled up in a corner.

But it will. Phil and Damon have a vision for this place. It'll be gorgeous when they're finished."

"How long will it take?"

"Matt's spending Christmas here with his girlfriend Geena, so Phil and Damon plan to have it ready by then." And his son would be due in January. He desperately wanted to spend Christmas with Tess but he didn't know if she'd allow it.

"You won't be living here then."

"God, I hope not. I need to get back to work. I was thinking I'd take some time off around Christmas, though." *Hint, hint.*

"I usually spend Christmas with my folks in Laramie." She made a face. "Although I might not be welcome this year."

"Why not?"

She swept a hand toward her stomach. "They don't approve of unwed mothers."

He'd had a solution for that. "Maybe they don't approve, but this is their grandson we're talking about."

"I know and I'm hoping that makes a difference, but they're very critical people. No telling what they'll read into this considering I couldn't get pregnant with Jared and then some tall, dark stranger comes along and bam, I'm PG."

He didn't think he'd like her parents much. "You can soft-pedal the stranger part and play up the Thunder Mountain angle. Throw in my movie star brother if that helps any."

"It would make things worse. They think of Hollywood as the equivalent of Sodom and Gomorrah. They firmly believe that good girls don't get pregnant unless they're married. I doubt I'll get a pass because I'm having their first and probably only grandchild."

So she'd rejected his proposal knowing her parents would have wanted her to accept. Obviously she wasn't a slave to their approval and he admired her for it. "Why would he be the only grandchild?"

"I have no siblings and I doubt I'll have the good fortune to get pregnant twice."

"I predict you'll be able to have as many kids as you want."

"Now there's a bold statement. What are you basing it on, pray tell?"

"Just a gut feeling." He hadn't known he'd say that, yet it felt right. Several things had to fall into place before his prediction could come true, but they were all within the realm of possibility. As she stood in the glow of the kitchen's soft light, he imagined her surrounded by her children. Because it was his fantasy, he visualized two towheads and two with dark hair like his.

He longed to close the gap between them and take her into his arms. Then he'd kiss her and promise to do everything in his power to make that picture a reality, including booking a room at their favorite Texas hotel during her fertile period. But since he couldn't say or do any of that, he came up with another idea.

"We have some time before the meal's ready," he said. "And my phone's charged. What if we spend the time looking up baby names?"

She stared at him as if he'd sprouted a second head.

"Or not." Apparently he'd just stepped on sacred ground. "We could play cards. I like playing solitaire old school, with real cards. But gin rummy's fun for two—"

"We can check out baby names."

"Are you sure? Because a moment ago you looked as if I'd suggested adding a side of grub worms to our dinner."

"I was surprised."

"I could tell."

"I assumed I'd be the one to…"

"You definitely get the final say. I'd just like some input."

She studied him for a moment. "That's fair. I should at least find out if there are any you hate."

"Elmer and Hubert. And I just realized I'm not crazy about Marvin, either."

She grinned. "You're safe on all of those."

"Then let's sit and call up a baby name site."

She picked up her purse from the counter where she'd laid it down.

"Do you have a list going already?"

"I don't, believe it or not." She dug out a small notepad and a pen. "I was saving it for later when I'm big as a house and we have six feet of snow on the ground."

"Look, if you'd rather not…"

"I want to. You're here and I'm here. We have time on our hands."

"True." How did that old song go? Something about time on my hands and you in my arms. He walked around and pulled out a chair for her.

"You have beautiful manners, Zeke."

"You can thank Rosie. She's a stickler. That's why I got in trouble for not calling you back. And I'm very sorry for that."

"I know you are. It's okay."

"Like you said, maybe it's better that you told me in person."

"Maybe." But she didn't meet his gaze.

He straddled his chair backward instead of drawing it up to the table where he'd end up playing footsie with her again. That had been way too much fun.

"Okay—" he looked at his phone "—starting at the first letter. Do you have anything against *A* names?"

"Not as a general category."

"Then here's one. Abelard."

"I can't tell if you're serious or not."

"Not. He would get beat up at school every single day."

"Unless," she said, "he went by Abe. That might be okay."

"Are you saying you want Abelard on the list? Because I can guarantee that his teachers won't call him Abe, especially on the first day. They'll say the whole blessed thing and our son's life will be a living hell for the rest of the year. I'm aware of this because my first name is Ezekiel."

"I never knew that."

"Which is how I prefer it, but you'll have to write my legal name on the birth certificate so I have to fess up. Ezekiel Manfred Rafferty."

"Manfred?"

"I know, right? Ezekiel's a big enough load for a kid to carry, but add on Manfred and you'd better hope he's either a scrappy little guy or too cute for words."

"Which were you?"

"Both."

She burst out laughing. "And modest. Don't forget modest."

He was making her laugh, and that was a good thing. They'd done a lot of laughing in that hotel room but they'd been too serious recently. "How do you like Andrew?"

"Not bad, but you've skipped a whole bunch if you're already up to Andrew. Just start with the first one and go through them all. That way we can—"

Lightning hit so close they both leaped up at the same moment the house was plunged into darkness. A loud crash followed, along with the crack and tinkle of breaking glass.

Zeke tapped the flashlight app on his phone. "Stay here. I'll investigate."

"I most certainly won't stay here." She pulled her phone out of her purse. "Two lights are better than one. Let's go."

"At least let me go first. I'm wearing boots and there's probably glass everywhere. I have a bad feeling I know what happened." He started down the hall. "There's a big tree in the front yard. I'll bet a branch came through the picture window in the master bedroom. I only hope it wasn't the whole tree."

"And that we can find a way to keep rain from coming in through a broken window."

"That, too." He reached the doorway and moved his light around. "Damn." A branch as big as his thigh had split from the tree and now lay across the windowsill. It extended about five feet into the room but, fortunately, didn't quite reach the bed.

Jagged pieces of glass littered the floor and rain from the broken window was already creating puddles on the hardwood floor. Good thing the floor was being replaced. Still, he couldn't allow water to accumulate and seep into the walls.

"Yikes." Tess peered around him. "What now?"

"I'm thinking." He took a deep breath. "Okay, first I'll get a tow rope around that branch and use my truck to pull it back out into the yard."

"I could guide it from in here."

"You might be able to, especially if you wear gloves. I'm pretty sure Damon and Phil left a couple of pairs here. At the very least you can yell out and tell me how I'm doing. But you'll need to be in the room and I'm worried about those flimsy canvas shoes you're wearing."

"I'll be careful."

"Not good enough. A piece of glass could slice right through those thin rubber soles. Wait! I have it. Stay here a sec. I'll get you some boots." The left side of the room was relatively clear of glass as he walked to the closet, hauled out his show boots and grabbed a thick pair of socks from the top dresser drawer.

He brought them to Tess. "Let's go back to the kitchen so you can put them on."

"Are those rhinestones?"

"Yes, ma'am. You saw the show. Don't you remember the glittery stuff?"

"I guess so. I was concentrating on your amazing stunts with those ropes. Are you sure I should wear these? They'll get wet."

"You won't be wading through a creek in them, so they'll be fine. And I won't be worrying about your feet."

When they got back to the kitchen he left to find some gloves while she took off her shoes and put on the heavy socks and his boots. He returned to find her standing beside the table, her flashlight shining on the boots.

"Do I look stylin' or what?"

"You look a lot better than the guy who owns them. But will they work?"

"Well enough." She took a few tentative steps. "I wouldn't want to run a foot race but if I don't move too fast I'll be okay."

"Here's some gloves, although don't feel you have to manhandle that tree branch. If you can help guide it through, great, but be very careful of the glass that's still in the window."

"Must be a really old window. All the broken windows I've seen shatter into a million little pieces, not those big jagged ones."

"I'm sure it's old. Be careful of the pieces on the floor, too." He had a sudden scary thought. "Is there any chance you'll fall down in those oversize boots? That would be worse."

"I'll make sure I don't."

"You know what? Let me do this. I can pull the branch out by myself. I don't want to risk having you injured in the process."

"Sorry, but that's not how I roll. You loaned me these snazzy boots and I'm going to make use of them."

"But—"

"No arguments, Ezekiel Manfred Rafferty." She reached up, pulled his head down and kissed him firmly on the mouth. Then she took a couple of careful steps back. "Understood?"

He was so shocked by her kiss that he didn't react. He just stood there like a man carved from stone.

"Now go lasso that branch and get it out of Matt's bedroom. I'll supervise from inside."

He snapped out of his trance. "Yes, ma'am." He automatically touched the brim of his hat before he went out the front door.

He was soaked by the time he made it to his truck. The wind whipped his wet clothes against his body so, technically, he should be shivering from the cold. He barely noticed. *She'd kissed him.* Hot damn.

Chapter Ten

Kissing Zeke might not have been the wisest move, but Tess hadn't been able to help herself. He'd loaned her his show boots to protect her feet. How gallant was that? She'd lived in cowboy country all her life so she knew what boots like these must have cost. They were probably the most expensive item of clothing he owned.

But he wasn't worried about the boots. Instead he was worried that because they were too big they'd make her clumsy and she'd fall onto broken glass. At this point she wasn't sure whether his concern was for her, the baby, or both, but she appreciated his gesture no matter what the reason.

Using her phone's flashlight to guide her, she clomped down the hallway and stepped into the bedroom. The wet tree branch sticking through the window looked a lot more menacing without Zeke beside her.

She put on the gloves he'd found and walked slowly to the window, glass crunching under the soles of Zeke's boots. He'd been right about her canvas shoes. Her feet would be bleeding by now.

Wind and rain came in around the branch. Once Zeke pulled the branch out, water would pour in. She used her flashlight to assess the opening. Sure enough, pieces of glass stuck out of the window frame like shark's teeth. She wouldn't be pushing her arm through there.

She heard the rumble of Zeke's truck and moments later his headlights gave her a better view of the damage. She could see the slash of bare wood where the branch had been ripped from the tree by the lightning strike. The wood was singed but not burning.

Good Lord, she hadn't thought about the danger Zeke had put himself in by running outside to get his truck. Lightning still lit the sky. Her stomach hollowed out at the image of Zeke lying unconscious on the muddy ground.

Suddenly, Zeke appeared at the window. Rain cascaded from his hat, and his shirt was practically transparent. "The strongest branches are inside." He raised his voice to be heard above the wind. "Here's the end of the rope. Loop it through some really sturdy ones and pass it back out to me."

She assessed the situation and did as he asked. She was getting wet, too, but nothing compared to him. Walking around the branch, she finished the job on the other side and carefully handed him the rope without coming anywhere near the shards of glass still in the window frame.

"Perfect, thanks." He held her gaze. "Promise me

you'll stand back while I tow it out. I'll leave my windows down so if you notice the whole operation going south, yell out. I'll hear you."

"It won't go south. You've got this." She gave him a thumbs-up.

His grin flashed. "Roping is what I do." Then he was gone.

The truck reversed direction, facing away from the broken window. She could hear him in the darkness securing the rope, and she smiled at his colorful language. If ever there was an appropriate time for cussing, this was it. The rope had to be slippery and even with gloves the job would be tough. But he'd handle it. As he's said, roping was what he did.

The romance of Zeke's profession had appealed to her back in April. Because Jared was an accountant, spending the weekend with a trick roper had been a walk on the wild side. Spending time with him still was. She couldn't imagine Jared going out into a storm to pull a tree branch from a broken window. He would have called somebody.

Zeke, however, put the truck in gear and hauled ass, as they said in cowboy country. The branch quivered, crackled and slid neatly out of the frame to fall noisily to the ground.

Tess made a megaphone of her hands. "All clear!"

"Thanks!" He switched off the engine and the next thing she knew he was back in the house and standing beside her. He dripped all over the floor as he gazed at the damage. Somewhere along the way he'd ditched his hat. "We have to do something about that hole."

"I know."

"But not until I take care of another situation."

She glanced over at him. "What?"

"This." Sweeping her into his arms, he kissed her.

She almost dropped her phone. She knew right away that this wasn't the kiss she remembered. Their relationship had changed drastically since April and so had Zeke's kiss. The mood in that Texas hotel room had been playful, exploratory.

But Zeke's hungry mouth as he coaxed hers open, and the determined thrust of his tongue, told her that playtime was over. He was extremely focused. And the most virile man she'd ever known.

Breathing hard, he lifted his head. "You kissed me before I went outside, Tess. I need to know what that means."

She wiggled closer to his wet, clammy body. "It means the same thing it meant in Texas. You turn me on."

"That's great, but I'm a simple guy, so I like things explained in simple terms. Let's say we get this window under control, clean up the glass and mop the floor. That leaves us with a queen bed that's available for use."

"Sounds like an interesting concept."

"The bedding will be damp, but I have spare sheets."

"The plot thickens."

"Oh, hell, Tess. Just tell me this. If I follow my instincts, am I dooming my chance to interact with little Abelard?"

"That's not his name."

"I know, but we don't have one yet so I have to use something as a place marker. Put me out of my misery. Can I make love to you tonight without worrying that it's a gigantic mistake?"

She wound her arms around his neck, being careful not to hit him with the phone she miraculously still held in her left hand. She gazed into his shadowed face. "It probably is a gigantic mistake, but we'll make it together. You won't get all the credit."

He slowly let out a breath. "Fair enough."

Giving her a quick kiss, he released her. "Phil and Damon left the plastic drop cloth rolled up in the room they were painting. I'm sure I've seen duct tape somewhere. I'll look for it if you'll bring in the broom and dustpan from the kitchen closet."

"As wet as it is, we'll need a mop and bucket."

"I love it when you talk dirty."

"Yeah, yeah."

"Are you smiling? You sound like you are. Too bad it's so dark in here."

"I'm smiling. That was cute. So where can I find a mop and bucket?"

"They're in the closet, too. I wish Damon and Phil had left their Shop-Vac but they took it with them for a project they're doing at home."

"No worries. Let's get to it." She switched on her flashlight app and started to walk away.

"Tess." His voice was deeper and sounded strained.

"What?"

He reached for her and pulled her close. "I'm going crazy. What if we leave the mess for now?"

"We shouldn't." Her heart rate picked up at the thought of abandoning everything for the sake of passion. "You'd hate yourself if you let this get any worse."

"Yes, ma'am." He cupped her bottom in his gloved hands and drew her in tight so she could feel how much he craved her. "But it would be worth a little self-loathing, don't you think?"

Her breath hitched. She remembered the pleasure he'd given her, could recall it in exquisite, panty-dampening detail. He had an amazing talent for choosing the exact pressure and the perfect rhythm to send her spiraling into a climax. No other lover held a candle to Zeke.

His grip tightened. "What do you say, lady?" His voice was low and seductive as he gave her a sexy nudge with his hips. "The bed's right behind you."

As her blood heated, her resolve faded. Maybe it wouldn't matter much if they taped the window now or a little later.

"The storm's letting up. I doubt the floor will get any wetter." A gust of wind blew rain through the opening, spraying them with water.

"What were you saying?"

Leaning his forehead against hers, he sighed. "Okay, so I'm wrong." He kissed her softly. "Soon," he murmured as he let her go.

"Hang on, I'm wobbly." She clutched the front of his soggy shirt.

"Uh-oh." His grip tightened on her waist. "Is something wrong?"

"Only that I'm consumed by lust and my legs feel like rubber."

"Oh, yeah?" He sounded pleased.

"Don't let it go to your head."

"Don't worry. It's going in the opposite direction." She laughed. "Saying things like that doesn't help."

"Which makes me kind of happy. I like knowing you're focused on my—"

"Stop! Talk about something else, please."

"Like what?"

"The weather."

"Okay, the weather." He paused. "Say, Tess, the storm really is letting up. If no rain comes in for a while, then we can return to my earlier suggestion."

"No, we can't. This is Wyoming. Just because it's stopping now doesn't mean it won't start up again in ten minutes."

"A lot could happen in ten minutes."

"Zeke, work with me, here."

"Yes, ma'am. You're right. We really do need to cover the window and take care of the glass and water on the floor."

"Thank you."

"Because pretty soon we'll be walking on it in bare feet. In fact, the rest of us will also be—"

"And I'm cutting you off, cowboy, before you get me all hot and bothered again. I'm steadier now. Let's do this." She pointed her flashlight toward the door. "Where's your phone?"

"Left it in the kitchen. Meant to grab it on my way back here, but I was focused on a hot woman and forgot. If you'll take the lead, I'd appreciate it."

His "hot woman" remark reminded her of another reason she'd been unable to forget him. She'd never thought of herself as particularly sexy, probably because she'd been raised by her strict parents not to think like that. Three years with Jared hadn't changed her opinion of herself.

Zeke was the first man who'd labeled her *hot* and his vision of her had changed the way she'd behaved during their weekend together. The mental makeover hadn't lasted, though. Back in the house she'd once shared with Jared and in a classroom full of small children, she'd reverted to her normal persona—an intelligent woman with average looks and a pleasant smile.

Finding out she was pregnant hadn't changed her view of herself, either. If anything, she'd denied even more of her sexuality. Mommies weren't sexy, or so her parents had taught her. But Zeke, who knew perfectly well that she was a mother-to-be, had just called her *hot*. And damn it, she felt hot! She wanted to peel him out of those wet clothes and lick him all over.

In the back of her mind a little voice whispered that surrendering to her urge was counterproductive to her original plan to raise the baby without him. If they rekindled their sexual bond, he might only stick around for her and not for their son. But wait—this was a man who didn't do commitment.

And that would make everything worse, wouldn't it? He'd be her lover until he tired of that role and a father to their son until that also wore thin. He might be good for her ego right now but he was a bad gamble for the long term.

By the time she'd reached that depressing conclusion, Zeke had retrieved his phone from the kitchen counter and gone off in search of duct tape to hold the plastic over the window. She found the broom, dustpan, mop and bucket in the closet and carried them to the master bedroom. The cleanup would be a challenge using only their phones for light.

No sooner had she thought that than Zeke walked through the door holding a battery-operated camping lantern. He'd tucked the roll of plastic under his arm and held the duct tape in his other hand.

"Where was that when we needed it?"

"Excellent question. Tucked away in the back of the kitchen closet."

"You didn't know it was there?"

"I knew, all right. But a certain woman who shall remain nameless has the ability to scramble my brain. I completely forgot about it. Herb bought it when I first moved in here. As he said, the power goes out all the time when you live in the country."

"I'm glad you remembered. It'll be a big help." And once again he'd reminded her that she was sexy enough to make him forget things. Heady stuff. He might be a bad gamble, but they were stranded here, perhaps for the entire night. If she thought she could resist him, she was kidding herself.

He set the lantern on the bed to give them maximum light. Then he laid the plastic and duct tape on there, too. "Since the rain's not blowing in right this minute, let's sweep up the glass first."

"What are we going to put the glass in?"

"I considered hauling the garbage can in here but I hate to. It'll be all muddy on the bottom after this rain." He rubbed the back of his neck. "I know. There's an empty cardboard box in the living room that Damon left for Sophie to play with. Be right back."

While he was gone she swept the shards of glass into a pile. The broom dragged wherever the floor was wet, but the glass had to be swept up before they could tackle the water. She went over the same areas several times though tiny pieces were probably still on the floor.

She glanced up from her sweeping when Zeke returned with the box. "Is there a vacuum cleaner of any kind in the house? I know I'm missing little slivers of glass."

"Afraid not." He put down the box. "I'll hold the dustpan for you."

"Why no vacuum?" She swept glass carefully into the dustpan.

"The Shop-Vac works fine for now." He dumped the glass into the box and crouched to get another dustpan full. "Matt'll probably buy a vacuum cleaner when he moves back in."

"Then we shouldn't walk around barefoot."

"Absolutely not." Glass tinkled as he dropped more into the box. "I'll carry you."

"That's silly." She swept the last of the glass into the dustpan. The thought of him carrying her naked was more arousing than silly. "I'll just wear my shoes."

"I'd rather see you wearing my boots." He dumped the last bit of glass and stood. His slow smile told her exactly what he was picturing. "My boots and nothing else. There's a fantasy any red-blooded cowboy can appreciate."

Normally she would have laughed off the suggestion and insisted shoes were more practical. Instead she met his simmering gaze. "Then I guess I'll be wearing your boots, won't I?"

He sucked in a breath. "Let's get that damn window covered up."

Chapter Eleven

The tape job wasn't particularly neat and definitely wasn't pretty, but Zeke didn't care. It would do the job. They'd stretched a double layer of plastic as tight as they could. If the wind blew hard enough, the plastic might rub against the remaining broken glass but it would take a while before the glass cut through both layers.

The repair only had to last until morning. Zeke thought it would. Good thing his right shoulder was uninjured. His left shoulder was bothering him a little because he hadn't worn the sling all day, but he didn't want Tess to know he was in pain. When he finally took her to bed, his injury was the last thing in the world she should be thinking about.

While he applied an extra layer of tape all the way around, she mopped up the water. The rain had started up again while they were covering the window and she looked as if she'd taken a shower with her clothes on. He probably looked the same.

He kept glancing over at her as she worked. They'd moved the lantern onto the floor so she could see where she needed to mop, and the light allowed him to do some unobtrusive ogling. Every time she gave the handle a firm twist to wring out the mop, her breasts quivered under her wet shirt. The shirt didn't disguise much. Either she was chilly or aroused.

She wrung more water into the bucket and looked over at him. "Are you finished?"

"Not quite. Why?"

"You're just standing there holding the roll of tape."

"Distracted by the view." And getting harder by the second.

"Watching a woman mop a floor turns you on?"

"It does if her shirt is wet enough."

She glanced down. "Oh." She pulled the material away from her breasts with her free hand. "Didn't mean to give you a show."

"And here I was hoping you'd intended to."

Holding his gaze, she let go of the material and allowed it to cling to her breasts. Her fully visible nipples tightened. "I didn't think of it, but better late than never."

His jeans grew uncomfortably tight. "That shirt must feel clammy against your skin." Her velvet-soft skin that blushed pink when he made love to her.

"It does."

"You could take it off."

"You said you weren't finished."

"Turns out I am." He tossed the tape to the floor. "How about you?"

Her blue eyes took on a devilish gleam. "I'll need at least another ten minutes, maybe fifteen."

"Wrong answer." He closed the distance between them, took the mop away and sent it clattering to the floor. "Finished."

When he swept her up into his arms, his shoulder protested but he didn't care. Her boots fell off her feet but somehow he avoided tripping over them as he turned toward the bed. "I promised you dry sheets. Is that a deal breaker?"

"Sure isn't." She wrapped her arms around his neck. "Takes too much time and I'm already wet."

"Is that a fact?" He was dizzy from wanting her. Carrying her to the foot of the bed, he laid her on the damp coverlet and followed her down. "Where would you be wet, exactly?"

Her voice was low and silky. "Everywhere, cowboy. Everywhere."

Ah, there was the sexy lady he remembered from that hotel room in Texas. "I might need to check out your story, ma'am."

Her saucy smile taunted him. "Please do."

With a deep groan, he took possession of her mouth while reaching under the hem of her soaked shirt so he could unbutton her pants. Only there was no button. Hallelujah, nothing barred his way except a drawstring. "Love the drawstring concept."

"Allows for expansion."

"Allows me easy access."

"Wasn't a factor." She helped him by wiggling out of her undies and pants.

"Is now." Sliding his hand between her satiny thighs, he sought the heat he knew would be waiting for him. "Sure enough, lady, you're wet everywhere."

She gasped as he began stroking her. During their wild weekend he'd discovered this was the quickest way to give her pleasure so he took the shortcut because he longed to hear her cry of surrender. In seconds she arched off the bed, her eyes dark with passion and his name on her lips.

As she lay dazed and panting in the aftermath of her climax, he pushed away from the bed so he could nudge off his boots and strip off his clothes. He felt as though he'd forgotten something as he helped her out of her shirt and bra and scooted her farther up the mattress. It wasn't until he leaned over her, his knees nudging her thighs apart and his heart pounding like a drum, that he remembered what it was.

On some level he'd known why this night would be different but the implication hadn't fully registered until now. As he slowly eased into her warm channel, he closed his eyes and shuddered in anticipation.

She cupped his face in both hands. "What is it? Why are you shaking?"

"You're pregnant." He gazed into her flushed face.

"Zeke, you won't hurt the baby."

"I know. But I've never made love to a woman without a condom. I'm shaking because this feels amazing."

She stroked his cheekbones with her thumbs. "I predict you'll like the experience."

"I predict I'll love it." Pulling back, he thrust deep and moaned. "Yes, ma'am, I'm definitely gonna love it."

Her fingertips pressed into his glutes. "I'm pretty happy about it, too, especially if you'll move a little."

Leaning down, he brushed his mouth over hers. "I plan to move a lot." He initiated a slow rhythm and groaned in delight. "And I thought we had fun in Texas."

"We did."

"But this is better. Way better." He nibbled on her bottom lip. "Thank you, Tess. Thank you for letting me make love to you tonight." He shifted his angle so he could reach her G spot.

She gulped in air. "You're very...persuasive."

"And you're the sexiest woman I've ever known." He increased the pace. "So proper, so quiet, and underneath that calm-looking exterior you're a volcano."

"Mmm-hmm." Her breathing grew shallow.

"Erupt for me, Tess." He braced himself on his forearms so he could watch as desire claimed her. Yeah, it hurt his shoulder, but who cared? Her second climax was usually more powerful than her first. "Show me the fire. Show me what you've got."

"Zeke..." She began to pant.

Now it wasn't just her fingertips pressing into his glutes. He could feel her nails. "That's it, lady. Go for it." He moved faster now and the friction was sweet. So sweet. She'd been responsive before, but now he sensed an untapped depth of passion rising within her.

"Zeke!" Her body bowed under him as he plunged into her again and again, coaxing more wild cries from her as she flung herself into the fire. Her energetic release triggered his.

The force of it shot from the top of his head to the tips of his toes, wringing a strangled cry of triumph from him. Gasping, he managed to keep from collapsing onto her as his brain slowly stopped spinning and his surroundings came back into focus.

He looked down to see how she was doing and she was staring right back at him.

Her lips formed the word *wow* but no sound came out.

He smiled. "You can say that again."

She mouthed the word again and laughed. "I wonder if pregnant ladies have more fun."

"Looks like it to me."

"And I'm starving."

"I'll bet you are. I'm hungry and I'm not even the pregnant person in this bed."

"We can't eat that meat loaf. No way it finished cooking before the power went out." She reached up and patted his cheek. "I'm sorry. I know you wanted me to taste it."

"Yeah, well, given the choice between a perfectly cooked meat loaf dinner and what we just experienced, I can't get too upset about how the evening turned out."

"Me, either."

He leaned down and kissed the tip of her nose. Then he cocked his head, listening. "Sounds like the rain's stopped, so here's an idea. When I found the lantern I also saw the Coleman stove Herb bought for emergencies like this. The meat loaf is done for, but I'll cut up the potatoes and use the Coleman stove to make country fries and scrambled eggs. Will that work?"

"You're planning to fire up that stove in the kitchen?"

"Nope. In the yard. You can sit on the porch steps

while I impress you with my superior camp stove cooking skills."

"That sounds fabulous except for the current state of my clothes."

"I love the current state of your clothes."

"Wrinkled and wet?"

"Gone." He flattened his palms on the mattress and pushed back so he could get a better look. His breath hissed as a sharp pain sliced through him.

"Uh-oh." She frowned. "Your shoulder hurts, doesn't it?"

"Not much."

"Stop putting pressure on it and come back down here."

"I'm fine." But he lowered himself to his forearms.

"You'd better not have reinjured yourself playing bedroom games, cowboy."

"I'm sure I didn't. Sometimes I just move wrong and the pain catches me."

She sighed. "I can't believe I didn't think of that when you suggested making love. You picked me up! That was not good."

"It's all good." He placed little kisses on her forehead and her cheeks. "Stop worrying about my shoulder so I can tell you how I plan to keep you naked a little longer."

"I'm not sitting on the porch that way, Zeke. Or naked and wearing your show boots."

"No, ma'am, you're not. I'll get a blanket for you to wrap yourself in while we shake out your clothes and put them on hangers instead of leaving them in a soggy mess."

"But I probably can't wear them when I go back to Thunder Mountain."

He gazed into her eyes. "You could stay." But he could see from the way she was looking at him that wasn't an option. "You don't want to."

"Not tonight. I'm Rosie's guest and, besides, it's… it's too much, too fast."

She was probably right, but that didn't stop him from wishing she'd said yes. "Okay. After dinner I'll loan you something to wear and we'll make the drive down the road in tandem. If you can get through in your car, great. If it looks like you'll get stuck, I'll take you back to Thunder Mountain."

"Thank you, Zeke."

"You're welcome. Maybe over dinner we can come up with a name for the baby." He left her warmth reluctantly and climbed out on the far side of the bed to avoid slivers of glass.

"We don't have to decide that tonight."

"I know, but it's fun to talk about." He turned back to her and almost lost his place in the conversation. Seeing her lying there in the lantern light, all rosy from what they'd done together, gave him a real high. "Don't get up. Let me bring you the blanket and the boots."

She propped herself on one elbow and glanced over to where they'd fallen. "I hate that you might have risked hurting your shoulder by picking me up, but… I sort of loved being swept off my feet."

"That was the idea. Now stay put. I'll be right back."

When he returned she was sitting cross-legged in the middle of the bed, finger-combing her hair. If he could make a video of that, he wouldn't ask for anything more. Well, not true. A video wasn't much compared to having the actual woman in his bed.

And this wasn't even his bed. At least the show boots were his contribution. He brought them to her and began gathering up her clothes. They managed to get everything on hangers with several kisses and fondling incidents thrown in.

Finally they made it to the porch, stopping for a towel and the stove along the way. She put down the lantern. "I'll wipe off the steps while you get the stove ready."

Although he had the urge to do everything for her, he realized they'd have food sooner if they shared the chores. "Thanks." He gave her the towel.

"You bet. The pioneer women did their part, and with the power outage I'm feeling sort of pioneer-ish."

"Ever live in the country?"

"Nope. Even though so much of Wyoming is rural, my parents aren't outdoorsy." She finished drying the steps and draped the towel over the railing.

"Then are you okay in the dark if I take the lantern with me to the kitchen?"

"Absolutely. It's nice out here now that the clouds have cleared away. I'll look at the stars and listen to the crickets. In fact, would you bring my phone when you come back out? I have a constellation app."

"Sure."

"This is a great setup, Zeke. I'm glad you suggested it."

"Me, too. Be right back." But as he gathered what he needed in the kitchen, he realized that nothing they were using belonged to him. He'd kept his possessions to a minimum on purpose, and it left him with very little to offer Tess and their child.

He made short work of chopping up the potatoes and whisking the eggs. He stuck a bottle of beer in one back pocket and a bottle of root beer in the other before carrying everything outside. Knowing she was naked under the dark green blanket, he'd have to be careful he didn't light himself on fire while cooking over the camp stove. He hadn't worked with one in years.

He handed over her phone and the root beer. After opening his beer and taking a quick swallow, he got to work on dinner.

"You look proficient at that."

He glanced up and discovered her watching him, the bottle of root beer dangling between her fingers. He would rather be kissing her than stirring eggs, but she needed food more than she needed kisses. "It's been a while, but it's coming back to me." He returned his attention to the stove before she took another sip of her drink. He'd have the urge to lick any stray drops from her mouth and after that, dinner would become a casualty of his lust.

"Is it like riding a bicycle?"

He chuckled. "Sort of. When I lived at Thunder Mountain, Herb would take a few of the guys for camping trips at the far boundary of the ranch. We'd hike out, packing our bedrolls and the food. Herb would drive his truck out there and bring a couple of Coleman stoves."

"Why didn't he just let all of you ride out in the back of his truck?"

"He was big on hoofing it every once in a while. Cowboys always prefer to ride a horse or drive a truck, but Herb wanted us to get some experience with plain old walking."

"He sounds like a great role model. Rosie, too. What a wonderful thing they did, creating a solid foundation for all of you and providing a place to come back to years later."

"Yes, ma'am." But he never let nostalgia overtake him. A couple of years ago they'd almost had to sell the ranch. He didn't count on it being there forever any more than he was foolish enough to assign the labels of Mom and Dad to Rosie and Herb. A mom could leave and a dad could die. He'd vowed never to make himself that vulnerable again.

"Do you walk much now?"

"Not if I can help it."

"So much for early conditioning."

"It wasn't early enough. I was fourteen, too old to convert to such things. Now you take little Abelard. If we encourage him from the get-go, then—"

"This Abelard thing has to stop. I'm bringing up the baby name website right now."

Her response tickled him. He'd used the placeholder name on purpose to get a reaction and then he'd added another layer of connection by saying "if we encourage him." She hadn't bristled. She could have missed the implication, or she could be getting used to the idea that both of them would be involved.

Maybe he didn't have much in the way of worldly possessions and maybe he'd have to continue traveling because he liked twirling ropes for a living. But he could still be a strong presence in his son's life if he convinced Tess he could make a valuable contribution.

This morning he'd been afraid that was impossible. Tonight he'd opened a crack in the wall she'd built around herself and the baby. He'd work on making it wider.

Chapter Twelve

Now that Zeke had shifted her focus to naming the baby, Tess was ready to get it settled. "You know what? Let's move past the *A* names. I'm not feeling the A thing."

"Because nothing can top Abelard." Zeke crouched next to the camp stove and stirred the eggs.

She appreciated having a man cook for her, especially one who looked so great doing it. "So true. I'm not feeling the *B* names, either, Maybe *C*."

"Clint?"

"Sounds like a cowboy. I'm not saying that's a bad thing."

He looked up and grinned. "Glad to hear it. But I don't see him as a Clint."

"Me, either. Don't see anything else in the *C* category. Moving on." She didn't come up with another possibility until she was going through *H*. "What about Heath?"

"Not bad."

She laid her phone in her lap. "Yes, but do you *like* it?"

"You know, I do." He paused, as if rolling it around in his mind. "I like it a lot."

A shiver of excitement zipped up her spine. That was usually an indication that she'd struck pay dirt, no matter what the brainstorming was about. "I mean, it works, doesn't it? He might turn out to be a cowboy or he might become a pilot or maybe a diplomat. The name would fit anywhere he ends up."

"You should see your face."

"What do you mean?"

"It's so full of happiness that I swear it's giving off light." He smiled. "And now you're blushing, so the light's sort of pinkish."

She was a little embarrassed, but pleased by his description. "I'm very happy talking about him and I haven't been able to until now because I felt you should be the first to hear the news."

"And now I understand the sacrifice you've made to keep the secret. Thank you, Tess. That's a gift, knowing I was the first person to find out."

"Well, you are, except for the nurse practitioner."

He waved a hand. "Doesn't count. I'm sure you have friends in Casper you wanted to tell, but you didn't. I can see why you're putting off saying anything to your folks, but when you got to Thunder Mountain you could have told Rosie. It's kind of amazing that you didn't. Rosie has a way of getting people to open up."

"I didn't come right out and say it, but I'm sure it was written all over my face, like now. She knew."

"Probably, but the point is, you didn't blurt it out. You waited until I showed up. Was that really only last night that you drove to the ranch?"

"Yes, last night. And I can smell something burning."

"Damn!" He pulled both skillets off the two-burner stove. "I forgot what I was doing."

"But we named the baby."

"We sure did, and it's a great name. He'll need a middle name, too, but let's wait on that, let the first name settle in."

"I'm fine with that. The first name's the most important, anyway."

"And there's no nickname for Heath. It is what it is. I like that." He dished the unburned eggs and potatoes onto one plate and scraped the charred part onto another.

"Me, too." She could guess which plate was his. "Listen, just do half and half. Give me some of the burned stuff."

"No, ma'am." He handed her the plate she'd expected, picked up the other one and his beer and joined her on the steps. "We had to skip the meat loaf and I just remembered that I didn't make the salad, either. The least I can do is give you the unburned part of what's left of our dinner. Now dig in. I know you're hungry."

"Thank you. I am." She started eating. "Tastes great, but I wouldn't have minded eating some of the burned food. It wouldn't be the first time I've done it. I burn stuff, too."

"I would have minded. You're my guest."

"For what it's worth, I feel very well taken care of."

"I hope so. Rosie will have my hide if I don't treat you right."

As Tess continued to eat, she thought about Rosie's excitement over another grandchild. "Do you think she'll like the name Heath?"

"Are you kidding? We could name him anything, including Abelard, and she wouldn't care. She says that decision is completely up to the parents."

"That's refreshing. Some grandparents want a say in the baby's name."

"Will your parents?"

"I wouldn't be surprised, but his name's Heath, and that's final. Before I leave, we can pick a middle name, too. I hadn't thought about naming him before I told them I was pregnant, but if it's a done deal, so much the better. That said, I hope Rosie likes what we picked."

"She'll love it. Mostly she wants a chance to hug babies and spoil 'em rotten. She goes bananas over Sophie." He finished the last of his food and put his plate beside him on the steps. "Speaking of Sophie, I should get my phone from the kitchen and text Damon and Phil about the window."

"I guess you'd better. Do you think they'll want to do anything about it tonight?"

"I doubt it. I'll explain that we weatherproofed it as best we could." He looked up at the sky. "Sky's clear, so it seems silly for them to come over and shore things up any more than we've done."

"Good. I agree."

He laughed. "You don't sound eager to have them pop over here."

"Much as I like them, I'm not."

"I'll take that as a sign that I've been a decent host."

"Or better yet, an indecent one."

He turned to her, a gleam in his hazel eyes. "Oh, lady." Holding her gaze, he took her empty plate and set it aside. Then he slipped his hand inside the folds of the blanket. "If that wasn't an invitation, you'd better say so, because that's what I heard."

"You heard right." She quivered as he cradled her breast and rubbed his thumb over her tight nipple. "But you have a phone call to make."

"I'll make it. But when I'm finished, where should I look for you? Back in the bedroom?"

"Not necessarily." Her breathing quickened as her imagination took over. "Don't you think it's kind of nice out here?"

He groaned softly. "Yes, ma'am. And soon it'll be a whole lot nicer." Leaning forward, he gave her an openmouthed kiss as he continued to stroke her breast under the blanket.

Tunneling her fingers through his thick hair, she held on to him and gave as good as she got. But when his exploring hand moved between her thighs, she scooted away. Gasping, she managed one terse word. "Phone."

"Yeah." He put some distance between them and took a shaky breath. "You make me crazy, Tess."

"So I see."

He gazed at her and sucked in another lungful of air. "It's been that way since the moment I saw you in that bar. I wanted to throw you over my shoulder and carry you off to my lair."

"What lair?"

"Exactly. No lair at all. I figured since my buddy wanted our rented room to be with his girl, I'd end up sleeping in my truck for the weekend."

"Instead I dragged you up to *my* lair." She smiled. "You weren't the only one consumed by lust."

"Lucky me." He reached out and stroked her cheek. "See you in a minute." He got to his feet.

"Want to take the lantern?"

"I can manage without it. I know where I left my phone. Be right back."

She watched him stride across the porch, so eager to get the chore finished so he could return to her. They still craved each other as much as they had in Texas, maybe more.

Imagining what was about to happen, she slipped out of his boots. She didn't want to accidentally kick him in the throes of passion. Then she peeled off the socks, too, because making love while wearing socks was plain dopey.

No question that lust had motivated them initially. Nearly everything they knew about each other had involved mutual pleasure. They'd had no reason to dig beneath the surface.

And she'd misjudged him as a result. She'd pegged him as a charming playboy, an expert in the art of seduction who sailed through life without a care in the world. The reality was far more compelling.

Zeke made her feel sexy and desirable, something no other man had accomplished. But lust was like a rich chocolate cake—tempting and delicious in small doses, cloying if that's all you had to eat.

And speaking of dessert, the creak of a door announced that her after-dinner treat had just stepped out onto the porch. She switched off the lantern. Making love outside in the dark seemed more exciting.

"Hey, why'd you douse the light? It's pitch-black out here."

"I'm right where you left me." She allowed the blanket to slide off her shoulders and leaned back.

His breath caught.

"I thought you couldn't see very well."

"I was teasing you." Crossing the porch, he came down the steps and stood at the bottom, looking at her. His voice roughened. "I can see perfectly."

"Then let me tease *you*." She pushed the blanket to her waist.

"Ah, Tess." He dropped to his knees on the step below her. "I think you like the great outdoors, after all."

"I didn't know if I would, but I do." Her heart pounded in anticipation of his touch. Being here with him aroused her more than she'd realized it would. She reveled in the silky darkness and the cool breeze that tickled her hot skin.

His voice dropped to a murmur. "Maybe you're a country girl, after all." He took her gently by the shoulders and pulled her into a deceptively slow, easy kiss. But his body vibrated with tension.

When she flattened her palms against his chest, she felt his heart racing. She tipped her head back and his mouth slid from her lips to her throat. "You don't have to go slow."

"I think I do." He placed light kisses along her collarbone and nuzzled the hollow of her throat.

"Why?"

He cupped her breasts in his big hands and leaned

his forehead against hers. His fingers flexed, massaging slowly. "I thought the second time...wouldn't be so intense. That I could take it slower, let you see I'm not some out-of-control maniac." He lifted his head and sighed. "But, God help me, I want you even more."

"I've never thought you were some out-of-control maniac." She pushed the rest of the blanket away. "Don't torture yourself." She gulped as sensation shot from her sensitive breasts to her core. "Or me."

Rising up on his knees, he released her breasts and cradled the back of her head, tilting it forward so he could nibble on her mouth. "I would never want to torture you. I only want to make you happy."

She reached for his belt buckle. "There's a surefire way to accomplish that." She had his belt partly undone when he took over.

After that, he didn't waste any time. Freeing himself from the confines of his jeans and briefs, he used one arm to support her hips and the other to cushion her back. His instructions were delivered in a voice tight with strain. "Grab my shoulders and wrap your legs around me."

"But what about your shoulder?"

"I'm fine. Just do it."

She wasn't about to argue. She held on tight, cradled in his strong arms. Then he was there, his solid length filling her.

Leaning forward, he feathered a kiss over her mouth. "Wish I could see your eyes better. I love how they look when I'm deep inside you."

"Wish I could see yours."

"Next time." He said it with such confidence, as if he had no doubt there would be a next time.

And how could she deny him? As he began to thrust, he gave her exquisite pleasure with each bold stroke.

Making love in the dark could have seemed anonymous, but not with Zeke. She knew the feel of him, the scent of him, the sound of his breathing and the sexy words he took delight in using as he coaxed her to surrender. No one inspired reckless abandon like this man.

"That's it," he murmured. "You're close. Let go. I've got you."

With a jubilant cry, she dived headfirst into a whirlpool of sensual delight. He followed a moment after, holding her close as his big body shuddered against hers. Eyes closed, she enjoyed the security of being wrapped in his arms.

He cared for her and wanted her to be happy. She didn't question that in the least. And in this special moment after they'd shared a wonderful experience, she felt something that hadn't been all that common in her life. She felt cherished. For now, that was enough.

Chapter Thirteen

Holding Tess while he listened to the crickets chirping, Zeke felt a soul-deep peace that he hadn't experienced in a long time. His shoulder hurt, but he downplayed the issue. What man in his right mind wouldn't?

As Tess grew limp in his arms and her breathing became light and shallow, he realized she might be dozing off. That was the other thing Rosie had mentioned when they'd talked about meat loaf. She'd said that pregnant ladies needed more sleep than usual.

He sure as hell wasn't letting Tess drive herself back to Thunder Mountain if she might fall asleep at the wheel. Really, he'd suspected all along that he'd be taking her in his truck. Trying to navigate the muddy road in her sedan made no sense. He'd figure out a way to get her car to her tomorrow morning.

But he couldn't take her wrapped in a blanket. Or could he? He hated to wake her up, and Rosie and Herb seldom locked the front door. They definitely wouldn't tonight, knowing Tess would be coming back. And they'd be in bed by now.

Slowly he eased her onto the blanket where it lay on the steps. Then he wrapped the loose ends around her. She made a cute snuffling sound but stayed asleep. After getting his clothes back together, he peered down. She hadn't stirred. This might work.

He went inside to grab her clothes, purse and his keys, then pulled her keys out of her purse and laid them on the counter so he'd have them tomorrow morning. When he arrived back on the porch, she didn't look as if she'd moved at all.

A wave of tenderness took him by surprise. He wasn't used to watching out for anyone but himself and, theoretically, he should hate the idea. He didn't.

She still hadn't moved after he stashed her stuff in the small back seat of the cab. He decided on another quick trip into the house for a pillow and arranged that in the passenger seat.

Finally he scooped her up and carried her to the truck. Getting her in was difficult and his shoulder protested the move, but getting her out would be easier. He'd never seen anyone sleep so soundly, but he'd never been around a pregnant lady before. He wondered if little Heath was sleeping, too. He didn't know how that worked. He belted in both mother and baby.

Navigating the muddy road from the ranch to the highway made him glad he'd done this. He was used to back roads without streetlights, but she wasn't. He engaged the four-wheel drive and plowed through the muck. Even that noise didn't wake her up.

Not long afterward, he parked in front of Rosie and Herb's place. The house was dark. When he opened the passenger door, Tess was still dead to the world. Leaving the truck door open, he moved as quietly as possible up the steps and across the porch. Sure enough, the front door was unlocked. He opened it wide and went back for Tess.

Getting her out was way easier than putting her in. As he cradled her in his arms and started up the steps, she murmured something and wrapped her arms around his neck.

He paused. "Tess?"

No answer.

Okay, she was still mostly asleep. The trusting way she clung to him when she was so vulnerable made his chest ache. The sensation was unfamiliar, but he kind of liked it.

Good thing he knew this house so well. Rosie had a night-light burning in the hall, which filtered into the living room and helped guide him, but mostly he navigated by memory. Rosie and Herb hadn't changed the furniture arrangement since he'd lived there, although individual pieces had been replaced.

He'd never considered that before. Maybe they weren't into rearranging furniture, but he suspected they'd left it the same for the sake of their boys. Guys who'd had rough beginnings would likely be comforted by familiar surroundings whenever they came back to the ranch.

Turning sideways, he maneuvered Tess through the doorway of her room and walked over to the bed.

Whoops. He hadn't realized that the bed would be made and he couldn't easily tuck her under the covers.

He came up with the next best thing. Laying her on top of the bedspread on one side, he reached over and pulled the far side of the spread over her. That plus the blanket should keep her warm.

She mumbled his name and snuggled into the cocoon he'd created for her. Crouching, he kissed her lightly on the cheek.

Her soft sigh tickled his face.

"I'll be right back with your things," he murmured.

"Mmm." She was clearly still in dreamland but might be vaguely aware of him.

He made the trip to the truck and back as quickly and quietly as possible. Leaving her stuff on top of the dresser, he backed out of the room and closed the door.

When he turned around, Rosie was coming down the hallway from her bedroom. She motioned him toward the living room and he followed. He should have known she'd be listening for Tess. Rosie had spent years keeping track of the comings and goings of her boys, and now Tess, mother of her second grandchild, was under her supervision.

In the darkened living room, Rosie turned and laid a hand on his arm. "Is she okay?"

"She's fine. She fell asleep at Matt's. I didn't want to wake her so I just brought her back in my truck."

Rosie squeezed his arm. "Good decision. She shouldn't be driving country roads on a rainy night."

"No, ma'am."

"How'd the meat loaf turn out?"

He'd expected a question or two but not that one. "We lost power partway through the cooking so we had to ditch it. I made eggs and potatoes over the Coleman stove Herb bought."

"In the kitchen?" She sounded alarmed.

"No, outside after the storm passed."

"Sounds like you had an adventure."

She had no idea. He was grateful the darkness hid his face. "We did. During the storm a branch came through the window in the master bedroom."

Rosie gasped. "Were you two in there?"

Okay, so maybe she had a better idea than he'd given her credit for. "No, ma'am."

"Thank goodness. Is it still there?"

"I used my truck to pull the branch out and we duct-taped some plastic over the window. It should hold until morning."

"Heavens. No wonder that poor girl fell asleep on you. Do Damon and Phil know?"

"I texted them."

"Well, then." Rosie heaved a sigh. "Thank you for getting her back safe and sound. I didn't think you'd let her drive back by herself." She patted his arm. "I'd better let you leave so you can get some rest." She stood on tiptoe and gave him a peck on the cheek. "Come for breakfast in the morning and bring Tess's car. Somebody will drive you back."

He breathed in the flowery scent that he always associated with his foster mother and felt a tug at his heart. He might not have distanced himself as much as he'd imagined. "Thank you, ma'am. I'll be here."

As he drove back to Matt's place, he thought about the crazy stunt he'd just pulled off. Normally he didn't get this elaborate in his dealings with a woman. Tess inspired him to dream up these scenarios, though. The morning's proposal had been a perfect example. In his imagination, she'd enthusiastically accepted, which led to some early morning sex on that flat rock.

Since then he'd learned more about Tess and understood why that never would have happened. He'd known of her previous marriage but hadn't realized the jerk had turned her against the institution completely. He still thought marriage was the way to go in this scenario, but since she didn't, he'd come up with alternatives until he found one she liked.

He arrived at Matt's ranch to face the mess he'd made cooking their dinner, but the power was back on. He scrubbed the burned food from the frying pans, ran the dishwasher and put away the lantern and the Coleman stove. He made a mental note to thank Herb for them.

The bedroom was a different kind of challenge. Even though he remade the bed with dry sheets, he felt Tess's presence everywhere, which made him restless. Damn it, he missed her.

Pacing the room, he argued with himself. He wasn't the type of guy who missed people when they weren't around. He enjoyed their company when he could and otherwise he was fine on his own.

Taking the barbell out of the closet, he did a few reps. Sure enough, he might have set himself back a little with his shenanigans today. He worked with the oversize rubber band some, too, and the doorway stretch the PT guy in Cheyenne had taught him. No worries. He'd get back on track after Tess went home to Casper.

Maybe that was the problem. Whenever he'd been involved with a woman she'd either been within reach or hundreds of miles away after they said goodbye. Since Tess was over at Thunder Mountain, she wasn't in either category.

He had a strong feeling she'd never fit in a category again. But while she was in Sheridan he would like it much better if she stayed with him. Rosie already knew what was going on.

Okay, that much was settled in his mind. Tomorrow when he delivered her car he'd ask her to move over here. She'd probably only stay another night or two, anyway, and he couldn't see the point in having her continue bunking at Thunder Mountain. Not when they had things to discuss and a middle name to choose.

Calmed by the idea that she'd be with him tomorrow night, he thought he might be able to get some sleep. But when he took off his jeans, something crinkled in his pocket. It turned out to be the list of reading material she'd given him.

If he had one of those books, he could read it until he dozed off. Then tomorrow he'd be able to discuss what he'd read, which might help convince her he was dedicated to fatherhood. But he didn't have a book.

Come to think of it, with the way things were going, he might not have time to look for any in town tomorrow, either. Even if he managed a quick shopping trip, he wouldn't spend tomorrow night reading. Not with Tess around.

Thinking about her lying naked in his bed erased all the calm feelings he'd had a moment ago. If only he had one of those damn books. Reading about pregnancy and childbirth would get his mind off sex real quick.

Then he remembered that a friend on the circuit read books on his phone. The process had looked awkward as hell to Zeke, but maybe some of the books Tess had recommended could be bought and downloaded.

Once he got the right app, the process was fairly simple. He chose a book that took him through the stages of pregnancy and explained the mechanics of giving birth.

The subject wasn't completely unfamiliar. Ranch kids learned about it from watching animals have babies. In high school he'd taken a required health course that had covered human pregnancy and birth. He'd never paid much attention after finding out how to keep a girl from getting pregnant. Procreation hadn't been his goal.

He doubted any guy on the planet had been more careful, yet here he was, devouring info about a topic he would have had no interest in two days ago. Reading on the phone took some getting used to, though. He kept wishing he could underline stuff or dog-ear a page.

He suspected there were ways to make notes on the book itself, but he didn't feel like taking the time to learn how. Instead he got a pad of paper and a pen from the kitchen and started a list of things he needed to ask Tess. It turned into a really long list.

Eventually he couldn't keep his eyes open. Then he spent the rest of the night battling nightmares about losing either Tess or Heath or both. He woke up early in a cold sweat.

He'd thought giving birth would be a straightforward process. Women had been doing it for centuries. What could possibly go wrong? Now he knew. Anything and everything could fall apart, sometimes without warning. And he was terrified.

He shaved and showered in record time. Stuffing

his list into his pocket, he grabbed the keys to her car and headed out. Phil and Damon would probably show up before he came back. No telling how long it would take for Tess to answer his questions.

Climbing into her car felt strange after all the years he'd driven trucks. He had to put the seat back quite a ways to accommodate his long legs. Once he pulled out onto the road, which fortunately had dried up a bit, he hated sitting so low to the ground. How did she get a good look at what was coming? He'd love to suggest she trade her car for a decent truck, but what she drove was none of his business.

He'd focus on the important issues, like whether she'd checked her obstetrician's qualifications. Now that he knew all the pitfalls involved in delivering a baby, he wanted details like how many years that person had been in practice and where they'd earned their medical degree. He could find out quite a bit online, but first he needed a name.

He parked in front of the house, adjusted the seat and shoehorned himself out of the tight space. The vehicle ran fine, but it seemed too small and vulnerable to protect the occupants. He wondered if she'd bought a car seat yet.

The comforting aroma of coffee and bacon greeted him as he opened the front door and headed toward the kitchen. "Rosie, it's me," he called out.

"Morning, Zeke," she called back. "Coffee's ready."

He walked in and she handed him a mug of black coffee. She was alone in the kitchen.

"Thank you, ma'am." He cradled the mug in both hands. "Where's Sharon?"

"Down with the kids. She's teaching them how to

make her famous French toast. I'm working on getting the students more self-sufficient when it comes to their meals. We have a couple of pampered ones who've never had to lift a finger in the kitchen."

"Speaking of that, what can I do?"

"Set the table, please. I have things under control except for that. Lexi and Cade will be coming down this morning."

"Should I set a place for Tess?"

"Definitely. She's down there helping Sharon, but she planned to come back up here to eat with us. I think that had something to do with your imminent arrival."

"That's nice to hear." He hesitated. "Rosie, I plan to ask her if she'll spend the rest of her time here over at Matt's." He set out silverware and napkins for six people.

She chuckled. "You'd rather not have to cart her back and forth while she's sound asleep?"

"Something like that."

"Every time I think I've seen it all, one of you boys comes up with a new one."

"Then it's okay with you if I steal your houseguest?"

"You can try. She has an independent streak. She might not go for it."

"I hope she does."

Rosie gave him a knowing smile. "I'll bet you do."

"And not just because of that! I read a book about pregnancy and childbirth last night and I have some questions."

"You have a pregnancy book?" Rosie had the egg poacher going so it seemed they were having eggs Benedict. She took a package of English muffins from the fridge and began loading up the six-slice toaster.

"Downloaded one to my phone."

She turned toward him, eyes wide. "Listen to you! I didn't know you were into reading on your phone."

"I'm not, but Tess gave me a list of books and I wanted to start on it last night."

Rosie gazed at him and nodded. "I see. What sort of questions did you come up with?"

"A lot." He pulled the list out of his pocket. "I need to know if she's aware of all the conditions that can affect the birth."

"Like what?"

He started listing them.

"Zeke, hang on." She shoved down the lever on the toaster and turned back to him. "Most of those things are extremely rare."

"But not impossible! Maybe she knows about them because I guess she's read the books she recommended, but I wonder if she's mentioned any of them to her doctor. And if the doctor has ever treated patients with—"

"Zeke, honey." Rosie walked over and laid a hand on his chest. "You need to dial it back."

"How can I? I thought having babies was a snap, but it's not. So many things can go wrong. A good doctor has to be prepared for anything and I want to make sure hers is."

"You're scared."

He sighed. "Yes, ma'am."

"You're a grown man and free to do what you please, but I think you're letting a little bit of knowledge spook you. If I were you, I'd hold off on that list for now, because you're coming across as paranoid, and you don't want that."

"No, I don't, but I want answers."

"Let's discuss this some more when I give you a ride back to Matt's. Until then I'd keep quiet on the subject if I were you. Just my opinion, but I think you won't do your cause any good by trotting out that list of questions."

"Paranoid, huh?"

"Yes, sir. Now, I hear her coming in with Herb, so put on your best smile so she'll know you're glad to see her."

"That's easy. I am glad."

Rosie gave him a fond look. "I know you are, son. I'm happy for you."

Chapter Fourteen

Tess's pulse reacted when she noticed her car parked in front of the ranch house. She'd been expecting Zeke, but expecting him and knowing he'd arrived were two different things. She hadn't been this infatuated with someone since she'd fallen for a senior during her sophomore year of high school.

Using the word *infatuation* was her new method for dealing with her increasingly romantic feelings toward Zeke. If she only had a schoolgirl crush on that gorgeous cowboy, she'd be able to get over it when he lost interest. Getting over it would become important when she'd have to continue seeing him because of Heath.

She hadn't mentioned to either Rosie or Herb that the baby had a name. She was a little shy about saying anything, even though Zeke had promised they'd greet any choice with enthusiasm. How could he know for sure? Sophie was the only example he had to go by. Tess loved the name she and Zeke had come up with and she'd be disappointed if it received a luke-warm response.

Rosie had said Cade and Lexi would be joining them for breakfast, too. Tess had met Cade yesterday when Herb had taken her on a tour of the barn. She could see why Cade, who had a sparkle of laughter in his green eyes, was popular with the teens attending the academy.

But it wasn't just his looks. Herb said they adored him because he obviously remembered being seven-teen. That made him tolerant of their behavior while still expecting them to achieve excellence. Cade had a reputation as a horse whisperer and Herb said the kids were in awe of his ability.

The academy itself fascinated Tess. She'd already vowed to set aside money every month so that when Heath turned sixteen, the lower end of the age range, she could offer him the opportunity. He might not want to take it, but with Zeke as a role model he probably would.

"Breakfast smells great," Herb said as they climbed the porch steps and walked to the front door.

"Doesn't it? I can't tell you how much I appreciate you two housing and feeding me for a few days. I'll miss the TLC when I go home."

"I hope you don't feel you have to rush off." Herb held the door for her. "You can stay as long as you want."

"Rosie said the same thing and that's very gener-ous, but I need to get back to Casper."

Herb nodded. "I understand."

She knew he wouldn't question her about her plans. Rosie would have found some subtle way to ask for more information, but Herb was willing to let things be. She'd only been here for a couple of days and she already loved them both and would miss them when she left.

But when she walked into the kitchen and saw Zeke standing next to the stove handing Rosie plates, she admitted she'd miss him a whole lot more.

He flashed her a smile. "Morning, Tess. Sleep well?"

"Like a log. You?"

"Not bad." He held her gaze and Rosie had to clear her throat twice to get his attention. He handed over the last plate. "Sorry, ma'am."

"You're forgiven. I think I hear Cade and Lexi. Oh, and Tess, that little silver carafe next to the big pot has decaf in it."

"Hey, thank you, Rosie." Tess hadn't committed to completely eliminating caffeine from her diet, but after discussing it with Rosie yesterday she'd decided to cut back. It was so like Rosie to act on that conversation.

Cade and Lexi came in and greeted her with enthusiasm. She wondered if everyone connected with Thunder Mountain was naturally gracious or if Rosie and Herb had set the example they all followed.

She'd bet those two had plenty to do with the fact that a newcomer instantly felt like a member of the family. It made perfect sense. They'd spent years bringing homeless boys to the ranch and giving them a sense of belonging.

"Hey, Mom." Cade walked over and wrapped an arm around Rosie's shoulders. "These sure are fancy vittles you whipped up this morning. I can't remember the last time we had eggs Benedict."

Tess slapped a hand to her mouth as the realization finally hit. Then she faced Rosie. "You made it for me, didn't you?"

Rosie shrugged, but she looked pleased, too. "You said you liked it, so why not?"

"That's…that's wonderful." She'd had a slight problem with being too emotional lately and now she was afraid she might cry. "Thank you so much."

Zeke came over and wrapped a comforting arm around her shoulders. "Yes, thanks, Rosie. What a nice thing to do."

"I thought this breakfast might be our only chance to get together and toast my next grandchild." Rosie glanced around at all of them. "Not with champagne, of course. The sun's barely up. But we need to celebrate the impending arrival of another member of the next generation."

"I'll raise a coffee mug to that." Cade finished pouring his and walked over to fill Lexi's mug. "Anybody else?"

"I need a mug." Herb opened a cupboard. "Rosie?"

"I need one, too."

"All righty, then." Cade raised his mug. "Everybody ready?"

"Just a sec." Herb poured coffee for Rosie and then himself. "Okay, go."

"Yeah," Cade said. "We need to do this before the fancy breakfast gets cold. Here's to…wait. Do we have a name? A toast like this is always more effective with a name."

Zeke looked at Tess. "Okay with you?"

"Sure." She decided Cade was absolutely right.

"His name's Heath," Zeke said. "We decided that last night."

Cade sent a glance of approval Zeke's way. "Well done. I like it. Let's raise a mug to Heath, the doughty offspring of Tess Irwin and Ezekiel Manfred Rafferty."

Zeke groaned. "Did you have to say all that?"

"You know I did, bro. The occasion demanded it."

"What's with the word *doughty*?" Lexi looked at Cade. "Where'd you come up with that?"

Cade's eyebrows lifted. "I know things."

"I realize you do, but I've never heard that word come out of your mouth."

"You will in the future. I just found it the other day and it's perfect for the brotherhood. We're all extremely doughty."

"What does it mean?"

"Stouthearted and brave."

"I'd never heard it, either," Rosie said. "But it's perfect for you boys."

Lexi gave Cade a soft smile. "Yeah, it is. I think you need to repeat your toast now that we know what you're saying."

"I agree," Zeke said. "It's great except for the part with my whole name in it."

"Okay, bro. Just for you. Raise a glass to Heath, the doughty offspring of Tess and Zeke."

Everyone shouted, "Hear, hear!" and took a sip of coffee.

Tess found herself getting choked up. Fortunately the next five minutes involved everyone taking seats and digging into Rosie's special breakfast. She didn't think anyone noticed her wiping her eyes until Zeke, who'd sat next to her, took her hand under the table.

"You okay?"

She nodded, still not trusting herself to speak.

He lowered his voice. "Were you crying just now?"

"A little bit. Zeke, your family is incredible."

"Yes, ma'am."

The meal was excellent and she enjoyed every bite. As she ate, she wondered whether Zeke had been asked yet to join the Thunder Mountain Brotherhood, that band of doughty men. She wasn't sure if he would do it even if they asked him.

As Rosie had said, he held himself a little apart. She'd noticed that Cade addressed Rosie as Mom but Zeke used her first name or ma'am. As Tess listened to the conversation around the table, she realized the same held true for Herb. Cade called him Dad and Zeke used Herb.

After breakfast everyone pitched in to clean up the kitchen. Tess was charmed by the custom. Obviously no man at Thunder Mountain felt entitled to duck out on household chores because of his gender. Tess almost wished Rosie had taken in dozens more boys if only to instill that value.

She gathered from the conversation that Rosie had offered to take Zeke back to Matt's. The damage to the master bedroom window was thoroughly discussed and everyone agreed Damon and Phil could probably use a babysitter today.

But when Rosie seemed ready to leave, Zeke asked for a moment to speak with Tess out on the porch.

She did her best not to laugh as everyone in the kitchen exchanged glances. Apparently an invitation to the porch was a significant event and they'd all give Zeke some privacy. She hoped it wasn't another marriage proposal. Surely he wouldn't try that again on the strength of some excellent lovemaking the night before.

Zeke wore his Stetson this morning and tugged on the brim as they walked out the front door. "This won't take long, but I didn't want to ask you in front of everyone."

"Okay." She turned to him and mentally crossed her fingers that he wouldn't make the proposal mistake twice.

"What do you think about staying with me for the rest of the time you're here?"

"Oh!" He'd caught her by surprise. "I'm… I'm not sure. That would certainly announce to your family that we're—"

"Rosie knows what's going on. I think everyone's figured it out, to be honest." He adjusted the fit of his hat. "I thought this would simplify things."

"You mean concerning sex?"

"Well, that, and we still have stuff to talk about. Lots of stuff." He cleared his throat. "You can think about it."

"Good. I need to. And just so you know, I'll only be here another night or two. It might not be worth moving my things over there for such a short time."

"Rosie said you might not want to."

She blinked. "You told her you planned to ask me?"

"I thought I should. I'd be taking her houseguest and I know she enjoys having you around."

"I enjoy being here." Silly as it seemed, she wasn't sure she was ready to leave Thunder Mountain and the two people who were becoming increasingly important to her.

"I admit Matt's place isn't as nice. There's no furniture to speak of. Phil and Damon may have to board up that window until they get a new one ordered."

"Oh, Zeke, that's not why I'm hesitating." She stepped closer and ran her palm up his chest. His uncertainty touched her. "You'd be there, and I hope you know how much I enjoy making love to you."

He captured her hand in both of his. "I sure thought you did."

"I do. But moving over there is like saying we're a couple and we're not."

"What are we, then?"

She gazed up at him and saw confusion in his eyes that probably matched hers. "We're Heath's parents and we…we get along great in bed. Beyond that, I don't know."

"Maybe if you stay with me we'll have a better chance of figuring it out."

"It's a valid point. I'll think about it and let you know this afternoon."

"Fair enough." He nudged back his hat. "I just need one more thing." He wrapped both arms around her and pulled her close.

"Should we be doing this on the front porch in broad daylight?"

"Yes, ma'am." Cupping the back of her head, he leaned down, covered her mouth with his and took charge.

Whenever he did that, she was lost. Rational thought disappeared as elemental need took over. She moaned and clutched his shoulders as the seductive movement of his tongue reminded her of the pleasure waiting for her if she agreed to his plan. When he finally released her, she was breathing hard.

So was he. Backing up a step, he braced his hands on his hips. "Maybe…I should've…done that first."

She held her arms close to her sides so she wouldn't reach for him. "Maybe."

"Tess, please say you'll—"

"I'll tell Rosie you're ready to leave." She wrenched open the door and ducked inside before she committed herself on the basis of one hot kiss. Everyone was still in the kitchen, laughing and talking. "Zeke's ready to go back!" she called out and dashed for the bathroom to splash cold water on her face.

By the time she felt calm enough to emerge, the house was quiet. She walked into the kitchen, thinking she'd get a cold glass of water from the fridge, and was surprised to see Lexi sitting alone at the table, writing in a spiral notebook.

Lexi glanced up. "Here I am, lying in wait for you."

"For me? Why?"

"I have this student who's only seven, and she's a challenge. Her lesson is today at two and I find myself dreading it. She pretends she knows everything and she knows nothing."

"Usually that's a defense mechanism."

"I thought so, too. Her mother's just like her. Bring up a subject, any subject, and this woman's an expert. But how do I deal with it when obviously the daughter's learning from the mother?"

"I have some ideas. Can I get you a glass of water?"

"Sure. Thanks."

Tess poured two tall glasses of water and joined

Lexi at the table. "First of all, chances are you can't keep the daughter from imitating her mother, especially at seven. All you can hope for is to make your time with her more productive."

Lexi nodded. "Agreed."

"So maybe instead of trying to teach her something she insists she already knows, what if you forget about the riding lesson and ask her to teach you something that she's good at? Something you need to learn for your job."

"That would build up her confidence, make her less defensive. Great idea, but what?"

"I'm no expert on horses, so I'm not sure. Brushing the mane and tail? Little girls love to brush hair."

"They do, but she won't believe I don't know how to use a brush. Hang on. I've got it. Braiding. She loves to braid. She has a bunch of those bracelets little girls make. She can show me how to braid the horse's mane and tail. I've never been much into that, so it's believable that I need help." Lexi laughed. "That's why I have short hair. Never did learn to fix it all fancy."

"That's perfect, then!"

"It is perfect. Thank you, Tess."

"No guarantees, though. Kids are tricky."

"But it's better than what I've been doing, which is engaging in a power struggle with this little moppet." Lexi sipped her water. "So the situation with you and Zeke is none of my damn business, but if you ever need to talk, let me know."

"Thank you. It's complicated."

"The Thunder Mountain guys are complicated. I realize all men are, but the childhood stories of the ones who lived here would curl your hair. That adds another layer of complication. This wedding you're coming to next month was years in the making."

"You've been engaged that long?"

"We've only been engaged since Christmas, but I've known him since I was fourteen."

Tess loved hearing about relationships with a long history. "So you're best friends?"

"Now we are, but it's been off and on since high school. He left for five years, worked on a ranch in Colorado, and then sailed back into town thinking I'd fall to my knees in gratitude because he'd finally decided to propose."

"Where do guys pick up these nutty ideas?"

Lexi shrugged. "Who knows? But obviously they didn't get the memo that a proposal doesn't fix everything. Not anymore."

"At least you know Cade can handle a long-term relationship. Zeke's never had one and now he's acting like he wants us to be a family. How can I trust that?"

"Are you asking what I think?"

Tess took a deep breath. "Yes. I'm starting to care for him. He told me about his dad, so I think he'll do right by Heath, but as for me…"

Lexi gazed at her as if considering her words carefully. "I like Zeke a lot. But if I were you, I'd be careful. Unless he fully commits to you—and you'll know if that happens—guard your heart."

Tess reached over and squeezed Lexi's arm. "Thanks. That's what I needed to hear."

Pushing back her chair, Lexi stood. "Just remember that everyone at Thunder Mountain is here for you."

"I know." Tess stood, too. "You've all been so welcoming. Rosie and Herb made it sound as if I could live here until the baby's born."

Lexi smiled. "That's just how they are—arms open to the world. Even if you and Zeke don't end up being a family, you still have one here. I realize you have your own parents but—"

"They're not like this." She swallowed a lump in her throat. "Nothing like this."

"Then I'm glad you found us."

"Me, too." She gave Lexi a hug. "Me, too."

Chapter Fifteen

Getting a ride from Rosie made Zeke feel fourteen again, except that his problems weren't those of a fourteen-year-old. "You were right about Tess," he said. "She's not sure if she wants to stay with me."

"I have a suggestion, if you want to hear it?"

"Yes, ma'am."

"Take her out to dinner tonight at Scruffy's. I don't know if she likes to dance but—"

"She does." He'd always thought they'd ended up in bed because they'd turned each other on so much slow dancing in the bar where they'd first met. "That's a great suggestion. Hey, you missed the turn."

"No, I didn't."

"What do you mean? You just passed the road to Matt's place."

"I know. I'm taking you to Sheridan Memorial."

"Rosie, if you're worried about my shoulder, it's fine."

"This isn't about your shoulder, although, if you want, I can have someone check it out."

"Not necessary. So why are we going to the hospital?"

"I'm taking you to the maternity ward so you can talk to my friend Joan who's a nurse there. Maybe you can even get a glimpse of some babies."

"What for?"

"You've worked yourself into a lather about the dangers of childbirth so I plan to give you a dose of reality."

Zeke sighed. "Rosie, you don't have to do that."

"Humor me."

"You're wasting your time."

"I don't happen to think so. Listen, Zeke, you've kept yourself locked down for years and now the thought of this baby is shaking you up. Nothing wrong with that. In fact, it's probably long overdue. I just don't want you scaring Tess with your out-of-control imagination."

He knew better than to argue when Rosie took that tone. "Yes, ma'am."

Twenty minutes later he walked into the hospital with Rosie, which was like being in a celebrity's entourage. Everybody knew her, apparently. The maternity ward turned out to be a cheerful place and Rosie's friend Joan was a skinny, gray-haired lady with a smile that took over her entire face. He couldn't help but smile back.

"So you're gonna be a daddy!" Joan said it as if he'd just won the Powerball.

"Yes, ma'am."

"When Rosie called she said you had some concerns."

Zeke glanced at Rosie. "You called in advance?"

"Of course. Joan is a busy lady. I wanted to make sure she'd have time to fit us in."

"Did you tell her I was paranoid?"

Joan's laugh was even bigger than her smile. "She did. I don't blame you, Zeke. First-time fathers usually go into this experience knowing very little. The process seems mysterious and intimidating, so it's easy to focus on a worst-case scenario." She gave him her bright smile again. "Wish I could show you one of our birthing rooms but they're all occupied."

"That's okay. I really hate to take up your time."

"Nonsense. I'm more than happy to talk with you. Where's your list?"

He fished it out of his pocket and handed it to her.

"Let's take a look." She moved her finger down the items. "This I've never seen. This has only happened once in my twenty years here and mother and baby made it through. This sometimes happens but it's an easy fix. Never seen this. Not this, either. This one's very rare and we have lots of advance warning."

Zeke's fears eased as she covered the entire list without confirming a single thing as a common issue.

Finally she gave it back. "I'm not saying none of these could ever happen, but the odds are good we won't encounter any of them."

"She's not having the baby here."

"She wants a home birth?"

"I don't know, but she lives in Casper, so her doctor's there."

"She'll be *fine* in Casper. Some excellent people

down there. Rosie tells me she's a smart lady in good health and she's taking care of herself. I think you can relax, Dad. Now let's go peek through the glass and look at babies."

Zeke followed her down the hall to a large window and there they were. Such tiny hands and feet. Their wispy hair reminded him of the feathers on a baby bird. Some slept and others were awake and staring at their surroundings. He could just make out their noises, which sounded like a series of hiccups.

"Cute, huh?" Joan said.

"Amazing." Zeke stood without moving, mesmerized by the newborns.

"All healthy with strong vital signs. This is the norm. Seven months ago Sophie was in this nursery. A good set of lungs on that one. She stood out because her hair was red right from the get-go."

"I wish Heath could be born here, too."

"I'm sure he'll be fine in Casper. You could go visit their maternity ward. That might help."

"It will. I'll do that." Zeke forced himself to leave the window because Joan must have other things to do besides escort him. If he was fascinated by babies he didn't know, how would he react when the newborn was his? He had a hunch he'd make a pest of himself so he wouldn't miss a single thing.

Before he and Rosie left, he thanked Joan and shook her hand. Not surprisingly, she had a firm grip. Then on the way out to the truck he thanked Rosie, who had known what she was doing all along. But then, she usually did.

They rode in silence for a few miles. He'd always

been able to do that with Rosie. She respected someone's silence.

But she did speak up as they neared the turnoff for
Matt's ranch. "Just so you know, I wish she'd have
Heath here, too."

"With Joan on duty."

Rosie laughed. "Definitely. Anyway, if Tess's parents lived in Casper, I'd say she needed to stay there,
but they don't and she doesn't seem very close to them,
neither emotionally nor geographically. I'm sure her
friends are great, but it's nice to have family around."

"I plan to be there."

"I'm glad to hear it. If she has him in January, the
academy will be in full swing. I don't know if I'll be
able to get away, but I might try."

"I know she'd like that. She thinks the world of you."

Rosie smiled. "Does she? That's nice to know. I'm
quite fond of her, too."

"Rosie, can I ask you something?"

"Anything."

"I've never stuck with a girlfriend for very long.
Two weeks might be the most time I've spent with one
woman. Do you think I'm capable of hanging in there
for the duration?"

"That depends. Why were your other relationships
so short?"

"I'd get restless and call it quits."

"Restless or nervous?"

"Nervous about what?"

"That you'd get attached to her and she'd leave or
die."

Her words sucker punched him. He had to catch
his breath.

"Sorry, son. I know that was brutal but Tess isn't just another girlfriend. She's carrying your child. These are good questions you're asking and you deserve good answers because the stakes are high."

He leaned his head against the seat and closed his eyes. "Tell me about it."

"Do I think you can commit to a woman and love her through thick and thin? Absolutely. I don't see Tess leaving you, but stuff happens. I can't guarantee she won't die."

"Women die in childbirth."

"I know, but I seriously doubt Tess is at risk. Can you handle a relationship? It all boils down to whether you can live with the possibility that she'll be taken from you. Or that the baby will be. We can do our best to keep our loved ones safe, being careful not to smother them in the process. After that, we have to let it go."

He allowed that to sink in as the tires hummed along the road. "How do you stand it, Rosie?"

"Stand what?"

"You love so many people—Herb, plus all your boys. Then there's Lexi, Phil and the other wives. The rest of us have started bringing more people for you to love, and now grandchildren are being added to the mix. Anything can happen to anyone. How do you deal with that?"

She pulled up beside Matt's house. "I accept the risk in exchange for joy."

As he absorbed her short but powerful answer, he met her gaze. "I don't know if I'm willing to make that bargain."

"That's up to you. But I promise you it's worth it.

Now let's go in. I want to see the window and I need some Sophie kisses."

Zeke was glad of that. He could use the time she spent entertaining Sophie to get himself together before taking charge of the little girl. He'd been kidding himself that babysitting while Phil and Damon worked was no big deal. By November he'd be back on the circuit and he'd figured the excitement of the arena would take his mind off Sophie.

That was a big fat lie. He'd miss her like crazy. He could imagine himself scheduling more trips to Thunder Mountain so he could see how she was doing. He'd want to be here for her first birthday.

He hadn't meant to let her penetrate his defenses but she had. Still, he didn't love her with the intensity Rosie did. That bond was precious and much stronger than anything he'd formed with the little girl. But when Heath came along…

Rosie had implied he had a choice whether to surrender his heart and soul. But he'd seen those vulnerable little newborns. He wouldn't have a choice with his son.

So he already had one hostage to fate, as he'd heard it described. He could either try to contain the damage or surrender his heart and soul to his child's mother, creating two hostages to fate. Every instinct warned him against it.

He'd known guys on the circuit who weren't with the mothers of their children. They maintained a cordial but distant relationship with the women so they could see their kids. These unattached guys were free to enjoy the charms of any ladies they met as they moved from town to town.

Zeke could probably work the same program. It would be similar to how he used to live and he'd been happy with that routine. So why did it seem so depressing now? The thought of hitting on some attractive woman in a bar left him cold.

Yet when he imagined dancing with Tess at Scruffy's tonight, he perked right up. He hadn't danced with anybody since that weekend with Tess. It just hadn't appealed to him.

He grabbed his phone and walked outside so he'd have a little privacy for calling her.

"Hi, Zeke." She sounded wary.

He understood. He'd left the ball in her court and she might think he was becoming a pest. "Sorry to bother you, but Rosie had a suggestion and I wanted to run it past you." He'd considered claiming the idea as his own but at the last minute he'd decided attaching Rosie's name to it might be better.

"All right."

"There's a friendly bar in town called Scruffy's. They serve dinner and they have live music and a dance floor. Would you like to go tonight?"

"I would." She sounded happy, too. "That's a great idea. Thank you and thank Rosie. I haven't been dancing since…well, since Texas."

"Neither have I. So how about I pick you up at six? And if you've decided to stay with me, I can take your suitcase then."

Dead silence.

"I see that last suggestion went over like a lead balloon."

"Was that part of Rosie's idea, that you could scoop

up my suitcase at the same time you picked me up for dinner and dancing?"

"No. That was my addition to the plan. So scratch that. I'll pick you up at six."

"Or I can meet you at Scruffy's."

Just like that, the wheels were coming off his romantic evening. But he'd take what he could get. "If you want to. Although I feel obliged to point out that meeting a date at the venue is not the cowboy way."

"I get that, Zeke. As I've said before, you have beautiful manners. But I'm not sure yet whether moving my things over there is the right thing to do. Plus, not having my car would feel claustrophobic."

Looking at it from her perspective, he could see why. "That's fair. I don't like being stuck without transportation, either."

"I'll follow you back in any case. I know myself. After dancing with you I'll be ready to follow you anywhere."

He smiled. "Good to know." This might work out, after all.

"But I still have to think about whether to stay there for the next couple of days."

"Understood. See you tonight." After he disconnected, his first thought was about the road. Some thunderheads were building up over the mountains and now she'd be driving her sedan over here and back.

He needed a quick fix for that low place in the driveway. If he called in the next hour he might be able to get a dump truck out here to lay down a load of gravel in that one area. He wanted things to go without a hitch tonight.

He'd been pacing the front yard during his call to

Tess, but now he sat on the porch steps to think. He'd made love to her on these steps. Making love to Tess gave him joy. He'd never felt closer to another human being than when he was intimately connected with her.

Even better, he could tell the feeling was mutual. Taking pleasure in the experience was fun, but giving it to each other turned sexual satisfaction into something much better. Something joyful. He'd never broken it down like that before.

The front door opened behind him and he looked over his shoulder expecting Rosie. Instead, it was Damon.

"Hey, bro." He took a seat beside Zeke. "Hope I'm not interrupting."

"Nope. Just thinking about something Rosie said to me."

"Yeah?"

"I asked how she kept from going crazy knowing anyone she loved could be wiped out in an instant."

"And what did she say?"

"She exchanges risk for joy."

"Wow. Someone should needlepoint that on a pillow."

Zeke laughed, which siphoned off a bunch of tension. "Thanks. I needed that."

"I could tell. You looked like you were carrying a Black Angus bull on your shoulders."

"Just trying to figure out what the hell to do about Tess."

"She has something to say about that, too, you know. It's not all up to you."

Zeke stared out into the yard. "I'm aware." He turned to Damon. "On a practical matter, do you think

Matt would care if I order up a load of gravel for the bad spot in the road? I'll pay for it. Tess's car can't handle that dip when it rains."

"I can't imagine Matt would care if you make an improvement to his road. He might even pay for it."

"No, this is my deal. I'll see if I can get somebody out here this afternoon."

"Sounds good to me." Damon cleared his throat. "Not to change the subject, but Cade called me this morning and we both concluded we've been remiss."

Zeke looked over at him. "Regarding what?"

"Ezekiel Manfred Rafferty, you're hereby invited to join the Thunder Mountain Brotherhood."

"What?"

"Cade and I realized you were off twirling ropes and such when we decided everyone who'd ever lived at Thunder Mountain should be considered a member. So if you wanna be in, you're in. If you don't, that's cool."

Zeke stared at him as feelings of envy and loneliness bubbled up from wherever he'd buried them long ago. Cade, Damon and Finn had formed the brotherhood a couple of years before Zeke had arrived at the ranch. They'd kept it exclusive to the three of them and Zeke had pretended he didn't care.

"We were jerks back then. Arrogant jerks. You have every right to tell me to take a flying leap, but I hope you don't."

Zeke found his voice. "Didn't you guys have some kind of oath?"

"We did. Cade made it up."

"What is it?"

"Let's see if I can remember. Okay, here goes." He cleared his throat. "'We swear to be straight with everyone and protect the weak. Bound by blood, we declare ourselves the Thunder Mountain Brotherhood. Loyalty above all.'" He glanced at Zeke. "You don't have to do the blood brother thing with the knife and all."

"Good, because I faint at the sight of blood."

"So you're in?"

"I'm thinking. What does *loyalty above all* mean exactly?"

"Bottom line, we'd protect each other with our lives." Damon wasn't smiling. "We're family." He met Zeke's gaze. "You can let me know." Getting to his feet, he put a hand on Zeke's shoulder. "And that 'trading risk for joy' thing? Mom's got it right, bro." Then he went inside.

Yearning battled fear. First Tess had punched a hole in his defenses by announcing she was pregnant. Now Damon had ripped away another chunk by offering him official brotherhood status. If he accepted that, his protective shell would be gone for good.

Chapter Sixteen

Tess found a parking space near the entrance to Scruffy's. Leaving Rosie and Herb's had been harder than she'd expected. She'd felt at home there from the moment she'd walked in the door, more so than anywhere she'd lived, including the house where she'd grown up.

But Zeke was right that they should make some decisions. They needed time together to work out their future plans. Sure, they'd also make love, and she looked forward to that. She was only human.

The main reason to stay with Zeke, though, was to get down to the nitty-gritty of how they'd co-parent this child. For starters, they needed a visitation schedule. She'd brought a notebook to record the rodeo events where Zeke expected to perform and the dates when he'd be able to make it to Casper.

The reality that he'd show up every few weeks hadn't sunk in yet. Would she let him stay at her house? Logically he'd spend more time with the baby if he did, but he'd be sleeping under her roof. She could guess how that would turn out.

Nothing about this situation was neat or structured and she *hated* that. The visitation schedule was a beginning, though. Once that was in place, she could talk to him about sleeping arrangements.

Someone tapped on her window and she looked over to see Zeke standing there, thumbs hooked in his belt loops in typical cowboy fashion. She turned on the auxiliary power and rolled down the window. "I was thinking."

"I could tell. I've been here for about five minutes and I finally decided to check on you and find out if you'd be coming out anytime soon." He gave her a crooked smile. "If not, I might go grab myself a beer."

Oh, yes, he was charming. One glance at that sexy grin and she was ready to order their meal to go so they could head back to Matt's place for some private time.

But she wouldn't do that. For one thing, he'd spruced up for this date. She could smell the citrus scent of his aftershave and both his shirt and jeans looked fairly new. The pearl-colored yoked shirt emphasized the breadth of his shoulders and the width of his chest. His belt looked hand-tooled and the shiny buckle might be a roping prize.

It would be selfish of her to keep all that male beauty to herself. She'd spent one evening with him in a bar before and she knew he'd collect admiring glances from the women customers now. If the servers were female, he'd get excellent service, too. She'd never seen him signal for another glass of beer. His level would get low and along would come the cocktail waitress to ask if he needed a refill.

"I'll come in." She buzzed up the window and pulled the keys out of the ignition. Before she could reach for the door handle, he opened it and offered his hand.

"Allow me."

"Thank you." Grabbing her purse from the passenger seat, she stepped out of the car and straight into his arms. He engineered it with such precision that it was almost like a dance step. She gazed into his eyes, which were shadowed by the brim of his black Stetson. "You smell delicious."

"I taste even better." He tilted her chin up. "But I'm not going to kiss you. I'll mess up your lipstick if I do."

The heat of his body called to her. "Ask me if I care."

"I like your attitude, lady." His voice grew husky. "I like it a lot."

"Wait until you sample the rest of me."

He groaned. "Maybe we should skip this and pick up a pizza."

"No, we'll go in. I want to dance with you."

"I have tunes on my phone."

"Not the same."

"Okay, we'll go in, but before we do, I have to ask. From the way you're acting I think I know the answer, but did you bring—?"

"In the trunk."

He sucked in a breath and crushed her against his muscled body. "Thank God. Now I really want to kiss you."

"Go ahead."

"No, ma'am. After last night's dinner, you deserve

to be fed right." He released her with obvious reluctance. "Let's go eat."

"Just so you know, I'm not starving. I had iced tea and freshly baked chocolate chip cookies with Rosie this afternoon." She'd hang on to the memory of that warm chat for times when she felt lonely or discouraged back in Casper. "She gave me some cookies to bring over to your place."

"That's Rosie for you. Always doing something nice for someone." Zeke took her hand as they walked toward the lighted entrance. Scruffy's had a log-cabin exterior similar to the ones in the meadow at Thunder Mountain.

"I can see why you like this place," she said. "It probably reminds you of home."

"If you mean the ranch, yes, it does. But I don't think of Thunder Mountain as home."

"You don't?"

"I don't think of any place as home. The ranch is great and so are Rosie and Herb, but I didn't actually grow up there and they're not my parents."

"They're not Cade's parents, either, yet he calls them Mom and Dad."

"That's up to him. Like I said, they're not my parents."

His jaw was tight, so she dropped the subject. What he called Rosie and Herb was none of her business. Whether he considered Thunder Mountain his home or didn't wasn't any of her business, either.

The mention of home and family clearly was an emotional trigger for him, and no wonder after what he'd been through with his parents. But that also meant she couldn't expect him to commit to her when she represented everything he feared. As Lexi had said, she'd better guard her heart.

Scruffy's was busy and cheerful, exactly what she would have expected from a small-town bar. They were seated in a booth. As she looked the laminated menu over, she tapped her foot to the fiddle and guitar music coming from the raised platform.

Zeke glanced up from his menu. "The band's good tonight."

"They're excellent. Can't wait to get out there."

"Since you said you weren't starving, want to dance now and order later?"

"Great idea."

"Then come on." He led her to the dance floor and spun her into a lively two-step.

They'd made it halfway around the floor when she had a horrible thought. "Is all this hard on your shoulder?"

"Could be if I didn't do it right." He winked at her. "But I do it right."

She had to agree with him. She'd forgotten how good he was. Her most vivid memory was slow dancing toward the end of the evening while they turned each other on. But that night had started out like this, executing elaborate steps and laughing as they navigated the crowded floor effortlessly. Dancing with a skilled partner was the best kind of foreplay.

When they returned to the booth she was breathing hard but far more relaxed than she'd been all day. "That was fun. I'm glad we're doing this."

"Me, too." He returned her smile before picking up the menu. "And now I'm the one who's starving. Worked up an appetite yet?"

"I could eat."

Right on cue, the waitress approached. They both chose the night's special with all the trimmings and Zeke ordered a beer. Tess asked for a pitcher of water.

The drinks arrived quickly but the waitress warned them that the kitchen was backed up.

"No problem," Tess said. "We can dance."

Zeke glanced over at the band. "Not right this minute. They're taking a break."

"So they are. Oh, well, that gives me a chance to find out where you got all those cool moves."

He laughed. "Are we talking about dancing or something else?"

"Dancing!" She flushed. "I don't plan to discuss the other thing in the middle of a crowded bar."

"But we did in Texas."

She leaned toward him. "Quietly. On the dance floor. We were whispering. No one could hear us." But remembering that seductive exchange made her squirm.

He reached across the table and held her hand between both of his. "I can tell when you're thinking about that particular topic. Your eyes go from light blue to navy."

"I need to stop thinking about it. We're here to eat and dance."

"And at the moment we can't do either." He rubbed his thumb lazily over her palm as he held her gaze. "So now what?"

Until Zeke, she'd never met a man who could take her from zero to sixty in less than five seconds. But they both had to throttle down or they'd never make it through the meal. "We talk. Tell me where you learned to dance."

"I learned from Ty, one of my foster brothers. He got me aside one day and said if I could twirl a rope I ought to be able to twirl a lady around the floor. I wasn't opposed to learning a skill that would impress women."

"FYI, it works." So did the slow stroking of her palm with his thumb. She should pull her hand away but couldn't seem to manage it.

He grinned, which added another layer of sexy to his gorgeous self. "Dancing was one of the most valuable things I learned at Thunder Mountain. When Ty started giving me lessons, some other guys wanted in. Looking back on it, those lessons must have been something to watch. We were a bunch of guys who certainly didn't want any girls to see us stumbling around, so some of us had to dance the lady's part."

"Wish I could have seen that."

"I'm grateful you didn't."

"Where's Ty now?"

"Living in Cheyenne with his wife Whitney. You'll meet them both when they come to the wedding next month."

"Will there be dancing at the wedding?"

"Count on it. Rosie and Herb will pull out all the stops."

"Then I have dibs on you as my dance partner."

"You might change your mind when you see Ty's moves. I'm an okay dancer but he's great. So are you, by the way. Where did you learn?"

"My high school boyfriend taught me. We dated for three years so I had a lot of practice. We even entered some dance competitions. Won a few."

"And then what?"

She shrugged. "After graduation we wanted different things. He assumed we'd get married and have kids right away. I'd decided on a teaching career. The breakup was the right thing, but so painful for both of us."

Zeke's grip on her hand tightened imperceptibly. "Have you seen him since?"

"Sometimes when I visit my folks in Laramie we run into each other on the street." She could be wrong, but she thought Zeke looked jealous. If she were a different kind of person, she'd let him dangle a bit, but she didn't like playing those games. "Last I heard, his wife was expecting their fifth baby."

His grip relaxed and he went back to caressing her palm while he studied her without speaking.

"What? Is my mascara smeared? Sometimes that happens when I get a little sweaty."

"No, you look beautiful. I was just thinking that if you'd decided to marry that guy, we'd never have met and there'd be no Heath."

Instinctively she put her other hand over her stomach. "That would be terrible. At least, I think it would. I can't speak for you."

"It would be terrible. Three days ago I didn't know he existed and now I can't imagine a world without him. And he isn't even born yet."

She nodded. "Exactly how I feel, especially now that we've given him a name."

"He still needs a middle one. Which reminds me that I don't know yours. Or whether Tess is a nickname for something else."

"Tess is short for Theresa. That name's fine, but it

didn't feel like me, so when I was around six I changed it to Tess. My parents still call me Theresa, though."

"Sorry."

"It's okay. I'm used to it, but if my mother's upset with me she uses the whole thing, Theresa Marie. When I break the news about Heath, I'll probably be Theresa Marie for a while."

"How about if I go with you when you tell them?"

She was shocked to her toes by the offer, but once the surprise wore off, she was incredibly touched. "That's very sweet of you, but I won't subject you to that."

"Why not? You'll be subjected to it."

"Yes. But I'm their daughter, so it goes with the territory, while you—"

"Listen, if they're liable to be mean to you or say anything rotten about Heath, I want to be there. You shouldn't have to put up with that. We behaved responsibly and against all odds you got pregnant. We've accepted the consequences of our actions and are doing our best to make a good life for Heath. We have nothing to be ashamed of."

She'd always respected him, but that little speech increased her respect by several notches. Everything he'd said was true and she'd do well to remember it when she faced her parents. Knowing he was willing to be there to defend her if necessary was a bonus she hadn't counted on.

"Thank you, Zeke." She drew courage from the determination in his hazel eyes. "I haven't decided when to drive down there, but when I make my plans, I'll let you know. Maybe you'll be free."

"I'll be free. I'm sure someone would be glad to

watch Matt's place for a couple of days when they hear about the errand we have to run."

She nodded. "Good to know."

Their food arrived along with a second beer for Zeke. He picked up his fork. "Okay, so middle name for Heath. Whatcha got?"

She scooped up some mashed potatoes smothered in brown gravy. Pure comfort food and, boy, was she in the mood for it. "You'll think I'm kidding but I'm not."

"If you want either Ezekiel or Manfred, forget it. Not happening."

The potatoes were so creamy and delicious that she moaned in appreciation.

He pointed a fork at her. "And making sexy noises won't help your case, no matter how turned on I get."

"It's the mashed potatoes. These are definitely not from a box."

"No, ma'am, they're not. That's part of Scruffy's promise, good cooking from scratch."

"If I lived in Sheridan, I'd eat here two or three times a week."

His head came up and his gaze sharpened. "Have you considered moving here?"

"No, I was only saying that if I did then—"

"I'll bet you could get a teaching job here in a heartbeat. Rosie knows everybody in town and she'd help you."

She should have seen this coming. Of course he'd want her in Sheridan so he'd have the comfort of knowing Heath was being watched over by his foster family while he was on the circuit. "I can understand why you'd think that was a good idea, but I'm not doing it."

"Why not?"

"I own a house in Casper. A very nice house that Jared deeded over to me as a part of the divorce. I own it free and clear."

"I didn't know that."

"I've never mentioned it. Anyway, I probably will quit my job, but I don't want another one. I'm going to open a day care in my home. It has the perfect layout and a great location. After Heath is born, a day care will allow me to stay home with him."

"But if you moved here, you'd be close to Rosie and Herb, plus everybody else. The maternity ward at the hospital is awesome. There's a nurse there named Joan. She has twenty years of experience delivering babies. You'd be in good hands with her."

She stared at him. "And you know this how?"

"Rosie took me there this morning."

"Why?"

"She thought I should see how terrific it was."

"But there's no reason for you to visit this maternity ward. I'll be having Heath in Casper." Then she got it. They all expected her to quit her job and move to Sheridan. Nobody had come out and said so, but that must be what they all were thinking. Otherwise why would Rosie take Zeke over to the Sheridan hospital? The audacity of it left her speechless.

Then it galvanized her and she pushed her plate aside. "You know what? I'll just leave for Casper right now." She picked up her purse and slid out of the booth. "We don't have to be in the same room to work things out, Zeke. We can text and email. I'll be in touch."

Chapter Seventeen

Zeke caught Tess before she reached the door. "Please don't leave."

She glanced down at his hand wrapped around her upper arm. "I have to." Her voice shook. "Let me go."

"At least give me a chance to explain." He had trouble breathing. He hadn't had a panic attack in years but he could feel one coming on. "I think I know why you're bolting and I want to set things right."

She looked up at him. "I'm having this baby in Casper, Zeke."

"I know you are." He cleared his throat. "Rosie knows you are, too. She's already trying to figure out if she can manage a trip over there in January."

"Then why did she—?"

"Let's step outside." He'd become aware of people watching them. Although Tess wasn't known around here, he certainly was. He'd rather not share his private business with the whole town or have it get back to Rosie that he'd had an argument with a blonde woman in Scruffy's.

"As it happens, I'm on my way outside."

"I can see that. Will you let me go out there with you for a bit?"

"All right, but please let go of me."

He did.

"And don't think you can solve everything by kissing me."

"I would never think that."

"Yes, you would."

"Okay, maybe in some situations, but not this one."

"You'd better believe it." She sounded shaky but determined. "Let's talk over by my car. That way when you've finished explaining, I can leave."

He hoped to hell his explanation would be enough to keep her there, but if not, he'd have to let her drive away. That would be tough.

They reached her car and she turned to face him. "Go ahead."

He tugged on the brim of his hat while he gathered his thoughts. Then he took a deep breath and told her about the book he'd downloaded. He bit the bullet and admitted he'd been terrified that something awful would happen. "So I told Rosie and she made an appointment for us to talk with Joan. It was designed to calm me down, and it worked. It wasn't part of some devious plot to get you to move here."

"But you want me to."

"Sure I do!" He started to reach for her and thought better of it, shoving his hands into his pockets instead.

"Obviously, Rosie would love it, too. But she wouldn't try to manipulate you into doing it. She'd just say it straight out. Does she know about your day-care plan?"

"No. This is the first time I've mentioned it to anyone."

"It's a good idea."

"I think so, too." She peered up at him. "Do you have an e-reader?"

"No, ma'am. I read it on my phone."

"Do you normally read books that way?"

"No, ma'am," he repeated.

"So why didn't you just wait until you could buy them or borrow them from Damon and Phil?"

He rubbed the back of his neck where tension lingered, although the threat of a full-blown panic attack was gone. "I wanted to get a start on the list so we could discuss some things while you were here."

"Oh." Her expression softened. "And you ended up scaring yourself."

"The visit to the hospital helped. But if you wouldn't mind looking over that reading list to see if there are any other books like that first one, I'd appreciate getting a heads-up before I dive into it."

"I'll do better than that. I'll trim that list to a reasonable size. I confess I thought you'd get discouraged by the number of books and maybe not read any."

"I knew that, which was another reason to get started and show you I was serious."

"You don't have to prove that to me anymore, Zeke. I do think reading some of those books will be helpful, but even if you don't open another one, you'll be fine. More than fine. I can tell you care about him."

He let out a breath. "Thank you for that. It means a lot."

"I just needed to be sure, for his sake."

"Of course you did." He searched her gaze and found warmth and sincerity there. And maybe, deep in those blue depths, a tiny spark of desire left over from their conversation before he'd screwed up the evening. "I had another reason for downloading that book to my phone last night."

"What was that?"

"I couldn't sleep and I needed a distraction."

"You have insomnia?"

"Not normally. Turns out I missed you."

"Oh, Zeke." She cupped his face in her soft hands. "How do you do it?"

"Do what?" He didn't dare touch her and ruin everything.

"I was so ready to leave a few minutes ago and now..."

"You're not?"

She shook her head.

He wanted to pull her into his arms and kiss the living daylights out of her, but he didn't. "We have food in there. Do you want to go in and eat it, maybe dance some more?"

"Would you...could we come back tomorrow night?"

"Absolutely."

"Because what I'd really like, if it's okay with you, is have them pack up our dinner so we can take it home. I mean, to Matt's place."

"Done. Why don't you just wait in the car? I'll be back as soon as I can."

Whew. By some miracle he'd pulled his ass out of

the fire. As he hurried across the parking lot, he heard her voice in his head—*Take it home. I mean, to Matt's place.* He'd made a point about not having a home and she'd paid attention.

But hearing her correct herself was jarring. What had once seemed like a ringing declaration of independence—*I don't have a home*—now seemed wrong for a man with a child on the way. He couldn't manufacture a home out of thin air, but he could acknowledge the one he'd been offered. He could accept Thunder Mountain Ranch as his home.

That thought had an unexpected effect. He felt a loosening in his gut, tension that had plagued him for years letting go. As he opened the door to Scruffy's, he dragged in a lungful of air and was astonished that he didn't tighten up again. He walked in feeling ten pounds lighter. Was it just that easy?

Probably not. The tightness would come back and just saying that Thunder Mountain was his home didn't make it so. But if he could start thinking in that direction, he'd have a more solid base, a sense of identity he could pass on to his son.

A server promised to locate his waitress so she could bring the check and a few to-go boxes.

Waiting for her gave him more time to think. If he allowed himself to call the ranch home, would it always be there for his son? Sure, because Cade and Lexi would keep it going. So would Damon and Phil. Although everyone obviously wanted Rosie and Herb to be around for years to come, the ranch's continued existence didn't depend on them anymore.

He was feeling pretty darned mellow about the future by the time the waitress arrived. She insisted on doggie-bagging everything for him and he left her a big tip. Food in hand, he returned to the parking lot and discovered Tess's car was gone. Damn it! She'd reconsidered and concluded he wasn't worth sticking around for, after all.

He trudged over to his truck because what else was he going to do? A note anchored by his wipers fluttered against the windshield. *Meet you at Matt's.*

His heart leaped when he realized she wasn't on her way back to Casper. On the other hand, he couldn't imagine what she was up to because he'd locked the house up tight. Rosie and Herb had the luxury of not worrying about locked doors, but he was living on someone else's property and the place was loaded with valuable building materials that could easily be carted off.

When he arrived, her car was parked beside the house. Carrying the food, he walked around to the porch and paused. She reclined on the steps wrapped in a blanket and she had her phone's flashlight set to a strobe effect for some reason.

"Hi, Zeke."

"Hi, Tess."

"I thought maybe the house would be open but it wasn't."

"Nope. Not my property." He shielded his eyes. "Could you please turn that off?"

"Oh, sure." She switched off the app. "I didn't want you to stumble over me in the dark."

"Not likely." He put the bags of food on the steps and crouched in front of her. "But I'm curious as to why you didn't wait for me."

"I felt the need to offer an apology for jumping to

conclusions and messing up our evening. I keep a blanket in my car for emergencies. I decided this qualified." She tossed it aside. The light from the stars was faint, but it was enough to reveal that she was gloriously naked.

He didn't need more invitation than that. He took what she offered, reveling in her sexuality as she tore at his clothes. He kissed and caressed every inch of her he could reach. It was clearly make-up sex and they both gave themselves to the age-old ritual.

As they lay panting and spent in the aftermath of frenzy and need, he gestured toward the bags of food. "Dinner."

"I am *so* hungry."

He toyed with her breast and nibbled on her mouth. "We could take it inside and warm it up."

"Why bother?"

"We don't have utensils."

"I don't care."

"Then let's eat, ma'am." Their feast was blatantly sexual. They ate with their fingers, which required much licking and sucking. He chose to clean off her fingers, an erotic experience that ended in another round of mutually orgasmic lovemaking. Afterward they collapsed on the steps, sticky fingers entwined.

Zeke sighed in contentment. "All food should be eaten this way."

"Might be a problem in a restaurant."

"Then restrict it to the privacy of the home."

She chuckled. "Think of the kids."

He turned his head to look at her. "You're a spoil-sport, you know that?"

"Hey, let's remember who suggested we consume this food with our fingers while naked."

"You're right." He sighed. "If it had been up to me, we would have driven home in tandem, warmed up our dinner and then had boring bedroom sex."

"Sex isn't boring in your bedroom."

"That's what I like to hear." He scrambled up. "But we need to be sure that statement is correct. Let's go test it out." He pulled her up and wrapped the blanket around her shoulders as they hurried to the front door.

Which was locked.

Laughing, he went back to the pile of clothes on the steps and found his keys. About that time it started to rain. "Be right there," he said. "I'd better get this stuff under cover."

"I'll help." Wearing the blanket like a shawl, she quickly stuffed the food cartons back in their plastic bags while he picked up their clothes.

They'd barely made it inside when the sky opened up.

"Just leave everything on the floor." He dumped their clothes by the front door and grabbed her hand. "I want to make love while it's raining."

"Like the first time?"

She remembered. "Yes, ma'am. Just like that." He tugged her toward the hallway. "Only better."

With the window boarded up, the master bedroom felt like a cave. They were giggling like kids by the time they groped their way to the bed and toppled onto it. As rain pounded on the roof, Zeke made slow, sweet love to her. He ignored the painful protest from his shoulder—something to worry about after she left.

Maybe he could talk her into a couple of extra days, because this was good, so very good.

Afterward they lay side-by-side as their breathing gradually returned to normal. Zeke looked over at Tess, just able to make out her profile. "Good thing it wasn't raining like this earlier."

"Could have been interesting." Her voice had a lazy, contented tone. "Ever made love outside in the rain?"

"No, ma'am. Wouldn't mind trying it with you, though." A bolt of thunder rattled the house. "Maybe not now."

"No." Her soft laughter was nearly drowned out by the rain.

"We might have lost power again. Want me to turn on a light and see?"

"In a minute. I'm in that floaty stage and I want to stay there a little longer."

"Floaty stage?"

"You know, where you're so completely relaxed that you imagine you could rise up like a helium balloon."

"Can't say I've ever felt that way. Only one part of me tends to rise up." He made the joke because he wanted to hear her low, sexy laugh again. But he envied her ability to achieve that kind of deep relaxation. He'd been in a constant state of alert all his life. Now that he was about to be a dad, it would likely get worse, but that was okay.

"The middle name I want for Heath is Abelard," she said.

"Yeah, right."

"I'm not kidding. It's unusual and distinctive. When it's paired up with Heath it becomes cool instead of weird."

"I'm not so sure about that."

"Let yourself get used to it and you'll agree with me. Besides, it means *resolute* and I like that. I did a little research and someone with that name is considered a deep thinker. If he takes after you, he will be."

"Now, that's a joke. I'm not a deep thinker."

"Zeke, you most certainly are. I didn't realize that during our weekend together in Texas, but now it's plain as day. You think long and hard about everything."

"What makes you say that?"

"Consider the facts. As a teenager you made a conscious decision about how you wanted to live and followed through on that plan. How many kids do that?"

"I have no idea."

"I'm no expert, but I'll bet not many. And when this baby threw a monkey wrench into your plans, you started working on a solution. Ever since hearing I was pregnant, you've been thinking through various scenarios to find one that fits."

"Huh."

"Nailed it, didn't I?"

"Guess so. That's…sort of amazing." It was also unsettling. She was right on target about how he operated. He hadn't realized she'd been observing him so closely. But it made sense that she would after he'd announced that he wanted to be a part of his son's life. She'd been evaluating his fitness as a father.

Apparently he'd passed the test. He'd never have categorized himself as a deep thinker, but when she put it that way, maybe he was. If she liked that about him and thought it would help him be a good dad, so much the better.

"Are you good with Abelard, then?"

"It's growing on me."

"Let it simmer in that deep mind of yours for a little while longer. I think eventually you'll—oh!"

At her startled cry he rolled onto his side and reached for her. "What's wrong?"

"Nothing's wrong. I just… There it is again! Zeke, I just felt the baby move!"

Chapter Eighteen

Tess lay as quietly as possible but her heart was beating so fast with excitement that she was trembling. Gently she rested her hand on her stomach. "He moved," she murmured. "I felt this fluttery feeling, and then I felt it again."

"You're sure that's what it was?" Zeke propped himself on one elbow and leaned over her. "What if something's wrong? What if our lovemaking caused a problem with the baby?"

"I seriously doubt that. All my reading told me that sex would be fine, especially at this stage, but yesterday I called my obstetrician to be absolutely sure. She gave me the go-ahead."

"You told her we were having sex?"

"She's my doctor. She has to know everything."

"Everything?" He sounded horrified.

"If you're asking if I give her a detailed description of our activities, the answer is no, but we did discuss positions."

"Dear God."

She smiled. "I guess it's a good thing I'm having this baby and not you, huh?"

"Yes, ma'am. A very good thing. I can't imagine how I'd—"

"There! He did it again." She grabbed Zeke's hand and put it on her stomach. "Let's see if you can feel him."

He hovered over her, his hand resting on her belly. Nothing happened.

"Maybe he went back to sleep."

"Maybe." He began stroking her stomach. "You have the softest skin."

"Don't give up. And keep your hand still. If you move around, you'll miss it."

"It's just that I love touching you."

"And I'm rather fond of having you touch me. But right now I—oh! Did you feel that?"

"*Yes!* Yes, I did!" He sucked in a breath. "There it is again. That's *him*. That's Heath."

"It is. I know it is. According to my research, this happens a little later with most new moms, but this is exactly how the books described the sensation."

"So he's precocious before he's even born."

She smiled. "Guess so."

"Does it hurt you when he does that?" He rested his hand on her stomach in a protective gesture.

"Not now. My doctor said when he gets bigger it can be uncomfortable if he decides to practice his soccer moves in there, especially at night. She said I might have some nights when it's hard to sleep."

"I'm sure." He leaned down toward her stomach. "Hey, Heath, buddy. Take it easy on your mom, okay? Don't be kicking her at three in the morning."

"He must have heard you. He's quiet now."

"They do hear what's going on around them. I read that last night." He glanced up at her. "I want him to recognize my voice."

"Mmm." That made her heart hurt. She planned to spend most of the pregnancy in Casper getting her day care up and running. He had an obligation to be here at Matt's and then on the rodeo circuit. Heath wouldn't be listening to his dad's voice much.

"I hadn't thought about how you'd deal with sleeping as he grows. Do you normally sleep on your stomach?"

"You haven't noticed?"

"No, ma'am." He chuckled. "In all the hours we've been in bed together, I don't remember much sleeping going on."

Neither did she. "I'm used to lying on my stomach, but I've been practicing sleeping on my side."

"I can help with that."

"You have some sort of trick?"

"Yes, ma'am. It's called spooning."

"That sounds great except that in a couple of nights I'll be in Casper without a spooning partner."

He was quiet for a moment. "Look, I know you have to go back eventually, but why not stay here a little longer so I can help you practice sleeping on your side? What's the rush to get back?"

"I didn't pack enough clothes, for one thing."

"I have a washer and dryer. Or rather, Matt does and I have use of it while I'm here."

"Thank you for the offer, but it's more than running out of things to wear. I'm impatient to turn in my resignation at school and get the paperwork started to open my day care. I want to have it going strong by the time Heath is born."

"Who'll run it while you're having the baby?"

"If I can get enough clients to justify an assistant, I'll train her to fill in during that time. I don't plan to be unavailable for long, anyway. But none of that will happen unless I get my act together now. Every day that I delay could mean losing potential clients to another service."

"You really do have it figured out."

"I have my part figured out, but not yours. I thought we could talk about your schedule and work out when you'll be able to come and see Heath. Unfortunately, I left all my things in the car—my notebook, my suitcase, the cookies and—"

"I'll fetch everything. I think Heath's zonked out for the time being, anyway." Rolling away from her, Zeke climbed out of bed.

"But it's still raining."

"Not so hard anymore and the lightning's stopped. Cover your eyes. I'm turning on the lamp. Of course it might not come on if that strike hit a transformer like last night."

She put her hand over her eyes. "I should've piled everything on the porch, but that seemed kind of dopey. I wanted to be the only thing you saw when you arrived."

"Considering how you presented yourself, I would

have been blind to anything else, anyway." He snapped on the light. "Aha. We have electricity."

"That's good." Slowly she took her hand away and allowed her eyes to adjust. Zeke had opened the closet's sliding doors and stood with his back to her while he took out some clothes. She admired the view: broad back, slim hips, tight buns and muscled thighs and calves.

But now that she knew more about his past, she wasn't drawn to him for his beauty alone. Despite facing horrors that no child should have to deal with, he'd been determined to survive. She admired his iron will even as she recognized what forging it had cost him. He was a lusty man who enjoyed physical pleasure, but he didn't dare let himself fall in love.

He pulled on briefs and jeans and boots, then turned, a man's bathrobe in his hand. "Want to wear this? I'm not saying you have to. You're more than welcome to walk around naked."

"I'd love to wear your bathrobe. I'm basically a modest person."

"I know." He smiled and handed it to her. Black velour without a bit of color on it. "That's what made your plan tonight even better. Where were you when you took off your clothes?"

"Under the blanket." She got out of bed and put on the bathrobe.

"That blanket's a lot smaller than the one we used last night."

"And I doubt I was completely covered at all times. I told myself it was dark and, besides, nobody was here. I have to admit I like the privacy of country living." The velour swam on her. She snuggled into it, enjoying the scent of his aftershave as she tied the belt and rolled back the sleeves.

"Cute." He grinned. "It never looked that good on me. So where are your keys?"

"The car's unlocked, but let's forget about getting that stuff from my car. It can wait."

"I agree that most of it can wait, but I have a hankering for some of Rosie's home-baked cookies."

"Yep, now that you mention it, so do I." She walked with him to the living room. "They're in a tin in the back seat."

"Be right back with our dessert."

She stood by the open door and watched him dash through the rain until he disappeared around the side of the house. Moments later, lightning slashed across the sky and she cried out as thunder followed right after. "Zeke!"

"No worries! I'm okay!" The car door slammed and he came running back. Light from the open door glistened on his broad chest and his dark hair was plastered against his head. Flashing her a rakish smile, he leaped onto the porch as another bolt of lightning streaked across the sky.

She grabbed him and pulled him inside. Thunder like a sonic boom shook the house. "You almost got yourself killed for cookies!"

Tossing his wet hair back from his forehead, he laughed. "That would look great in the newspaper, wouldn't it? Man Struck by Lightning While Fetching Chocolate-Chip Cookies for the Mother of His Child."

"I'm really glad that story won't be running in the next issue. Stay right there while I get you a towel." By the time she returned with it, he'd taken off his boots and was in the process of exchanging his wet jeans for the dry ones lying in the pile of clothes by the door. Once again, he was facing away from her.

He hadn't heard her come in on bare feet. She stood for a moment and watched him, fascinated by his toned body. He moved with grace for such a big guy. After zipping his jeans he gently massaged his left shoulder.

She walked toward him. "I had a feeling you weren't telling me the truth about whether you'd put a strain on it."

He stopped and turned to her. "It's fine."

"I don't believe you." She handed him the towel.

He began drying his broad chest. "I leaned on it for quite a while during Heath's kicking demonstration. It'll be better soon." He began towel drying his hair but he used his right hand a lot more than his left.

She groaned. "I didn't notice you were braced on your bum shoulder all that time. Do you have any kind of ointment that helps?"

"Yes, ma'am, but let's not worry about—"

"Let's do. Please go get it. What's the point in pretending not to be hurt?"

He lowered the towel and gave her a lopsided grin. "If you have to ask, you obviously don't know cowboys."

"Then let's put it this way. I won't be able to enjoy eating chocolate-chip cookies if I'm sitting there thinking about your aching shoulder."

"All right, I'll go put some on."

"Up to you, but if you'll bring it into the kitchen I'll do it for you." Looking into his eyes, she could see the battle raging. He was so unused to having someone take care of him, but the part of him he'd denied still yearned for tenderness.

At last he sighed, almost as if in surrender. "That would be great. Thanks."

"You're welcome." She picked up the tin of cookies he'd set on the floor. "I'll set up our snack. What's there to drink?"

He gave his hair one last rub with the towel. It wasn't dripping anymore but it stuck out in all directions. "Same thing as last night. I'll have a beer and there's more root beer if you want some. Plus there's water, of course. I'd make you coffee but all I have is leaded."

She resisted the urge to reach up and finger-comb his hair. She didn't care to experience his reaction to an overdose of feminine concern. "Water's fine with me."

"Then I'll meet you in the kitchen."

Setting the cookie tin on the card table, she got a glass of water for herself and took a beer out of the refrigerator. Opening it, she set the bottle on the table. The thought of beer and cookies made her grimace.

When he came into the kitchen, he'd combed his hair. "This is the stuff." He handed her a tube of ointment. "It doesn't take much."

"Have a seat." She motioned him to a chair and unscrewed the cap. "Go ahead and start on the cookies."

"No, ma'am. I'll wait till you're done."

"I can't believe you're having beer with your cookies." She massaged the ointment into his warm skin.

He chuckled. "You can blame the good ol' boys on the rodeo circuit. They taught me that beer goes with everything."

"You guys must have a lot of fun traveling around together."

"They're a good bunch." He moaned softly.

She quickly lightened the pressure of her fingers. "I'm sorry. I didn't mean to hurt you."

"You're not. It feels terrific."

"Good." She squeezed out another dab of ointment. "I know you said it didn't take much, but this absorbs so nicely."

"Yes, ma'am." At the start his upper body had felt rigid and unyielding, but gradually he relaxed. Slowly his chin dropped to his chest and when she peeked at his face, his eyes were closed. In that moment she faced the truth – she was in love with him. And because of all he'd been through, chances were slim that he would ever love her back. He wouldn't want to risk it.

Ah, but he needed love so desperately. She wondered how long it had been since someone had touched him in a non-sexual, nurturing way. However long it had been, months or maybe years, he was soaking it up now. She decided not to stop until he asked her to.

Eventually he heaved a gusty sigh. "That's plenty. Thank you."

"Glad to do it." She replaced the cap and walked over to the sink to wash off the ointment residue.

When she came back, he got up and pulled out her chair. "That really helped."

"I hope so." She opened the cookie tin. "I hate to think of you getting worse instead of better just because I'm here."

"Whatever I've done has been my choice." He waited for her to take a cookie before choosing one. "If it means another week or two of rehab, then I'll deal with that."

"But I know you're eager to get back on the circuit."

"I've been thinking about that. Since turning pro, I've paid attention to my financial situation. Because of travel expenses, some venues I barely break even. Others provide a healthy profit. I've done them all regardless because what else did I have to do?"

She had a hunch where he was going with this. "You're thinking of cutting back?"

"Basically I'd pick and choose so I can spend more time with Heath."

"That would be good for him."

"And good for me. I have a torn rotator cuff because I've been pushing it. I don't want to ever be laid up to the point I can't play a game of catch with my son."

"That's a worthy goal, Zeke."

He sipped his beer and gazed at her. The wheels were definitely turning. "Look, I don't know how to say this right, and I'll probably mess it up, but if I don't throw it out there you'll just go ahead with your plan."

She'd been about to take another cookie but she changed her mind. She dreaded what he might say next. "I like my plan. It's perfect for me."

"Are you sure? Because from where I sit, it makes a lot more sense to sell your house and buy something here, a house that would work as a day care."

The relaxed mood she'd been enjoying disappeared. "You're talking about a whole lot of work for no reason."

"First of all, I'd help you every step of the way because the last thing I want is to give you more to do. As for reasons to move, my foster family will support the heck out of you if you move here. Shoot, Phil and Damon will be your first customers, and, like I said,

Rosie knows everyone in town. If she spreads the word, you'll be turning people away."

"I know a lot of people in Casper, too. I've been a primary-level teacher there for five years. I'm impatient to get started and I don't want to lose any time. I'd lose tons of it if I do what you're suggesting. Putting a house on the market, buying a new one, moving all my furniture, finding a new obstetrician—the list is endless!"

"But you'd have help, mine and my family's."

She shook her head. "Don't you see? If I do it my way, I won't need any help."

"I do see that." He rubbed a hand over his face. "Damn it, Tess, I felt him move tonight. He's real to me now." He held her gaze. "I know I'm asking a lot, but if you'd be willing to move here, I could be with you for most of the pregnancy."

"I understand why you'd want that, but we're only talking about a few months. Then you'll be traveling while I'm adjusting to a different house and a different town. I know your family would be supportive, but it *is* a lot to ask."

"That's not all I want to ask of you." He leaned toward her and reached for her hand.

"Zeke." She tried to pull it away, as if that would stop what was coming.

"Marry me, Tess. I want to be that little boy's father in every sense of the word."

She squeezed her eyes shut to blot out the plea reflected in his hazel eyes. His sincerity broke her heart. He'd completely accepted his responsibility as a father and in his mind that should include marriage. But he'd never mentioned love and she wouldn't take those vows with a man who only wanted to do the right thing for his son. If that was selfish of her, so be it.

"You said your folks are likely to be upset about Heath. Won't marrying me fix that, too?"

That stiffened her spine even more and she opened her eyes. "I already married one man to please them. I won't do it again."

"You're right. That's not a good reason to get married. I'm sorry I even brought it up. But Heath is a good reason. He can grow up with both a mom and a dad in the house."

"Who are you kidding? You'll be gone half the time."

"No, I won't. That's what I've been trying to tell you. A lot of that traveling has been a waste of time and money. I'll be more selective. I'll look for performance venues that are closer to home."

"You don't have a home. You said so yourself."

"I want to make one. With you and Heath."

That was a huge mental shift for him and, even through her heartbreak, she perceived that. But she felt like screaming at him. She didn't, though, because he wouldn't understand why she was so upset.

He didn't realize that a marriage of convenience without love, which was basically what he was suggesting, would slowly kill her spirit. That certainly wouldn't be a healthy atmosphere for little Heath. She couldn't explain any of that to Zeke. It wasn't his fault that he wasn't capable of giving her the love she needed or accepting the love she had to give.

She drew in a shaky breath. "I'm not going to marry you."

"Why not?" He looked confused. "We get along

great. I know you enjoy the sex and I sure as hell do. Moving over here would be a pain, but in the long run it would be so much better for us, for Heath and even for my family."

She noticed he wasn't inserting the word *foster* in front of *family* anymore, either. He was changing, opening up. Rosie and Herb might eventually become Mom and Dad. He was doing it for the baby, just as he was determined to marry her for the sake of the baby.

She looked into his eyes. "I'm sorry, Zeke. More sorry than you know. But marrying you wouldn't work for me." She pushed back her chair. "I need to get going."

"Going? Where?"

"Back to Casper."

"Tonight? Are you crazy?"

She shook her head. "On the contrary. I've never felt more sane."

Chapter Nineteen

Zeke followed Tess into the living room where she began gathering up her clothes. He couldn't take back what he'd said because he believed it was the right course of action. But he was willing to compromise. "Let's forget about getting married."

"Never considered it in the first place." She grabbed the last of her clothes and headed to the bedroom.

"Will you at least think about moving here?"

"No, I won't." She walked into the bedroom and shut the door on him.

"Tess!" He had his hand on the doorknob when he heard the lock click into place. "Oh, for God's sake. You don't have to lock me out. What do you imagine I'll do?"

"Nothing." Her voice was muffled. "I just don't want you watching me get dressed."

"What? I've seen every beautiful inch of you, touched every inch, kissed every—"

"Shut up, Zeke."

"And you liked it when I did!" His frustration grew. "If you moved here, you could stay with me until you found a place. We could be together. I could give you back rubs. I read in the book that backaches are common, especially in the later months when the baby's heavier. I could—"

"No." The door opened and she came out fully dressed. "That wouldn't work for me." She moved past him and down the hall to the living room.

"I don't get it." He trailed after her. "I don't understand why you'd rather stay in Casper by yourself when we could be enjoying each other over here."

"I know you don't." She picked up her purse and turned to gaze at him. Pain turned her blue eyes gray but her jaw was tight with resolution.

"Explain it to me."

"Can't."

"This makes no sense!"

"But it's what I have to do. I've been debating how to handle our physical relationship as we go forward. Obviously we'll be seeing each other whenever you interact with Heath."

His heart began to pound. He had a premonition he would hate what she was about to say.

"But we won't be having sex anymore, Zeke."

He felt as if he'd been gutted. He had trouble getting his breath. "Why?"

"It's how it has to be. I'll ask you to please respect that. I'll be in touch." She turned and opened the front door.

"Wait!" He almost grabbed her arm but at the last minute stopped himself.

She glanced over her shoulder. "Why?"

"It's still raining. I don't trust that road."

"I noticed somebody dumped gravel in the bad spot. It should be fine."

"Or not. You could get stuck." He picked up his keys from the floor where he'd dropped them so they could race to the bedroom. That moment seemed years ago. "I'll follow you at least that far."

"Up to you." She started out the door.

"Hang on. I think there's an umbrella around here somewhere. Let me go find it so you won't get soaked."

"No, thank you." And she walked out on the porch.

Muttering several choice words, he stepped outside and turned to lock the front door. By the time he was down the steps she'd already disappeared around the side of the house. Cold rain hit his bare arms and shoulders as he clutched his keys and followed her. A car door slammed and the engine started.

He jogged to his truck and climbed in as she backed out, going fast. He yelled at her to slow down but doubted she heard him. He reversed the truck and went after her.

Now that he thought about the gravel he'd had put down this afternoon, he wished he hadn't done it. He'd meant to smooth her way in. Instead he'd made it easier for her to leave.

Clearly he'd spooked her with his suggestion, but what was he supposed to do, just let her go ahead and set up her business in Casper? Then she'd be really entrenched. He could see why she wouldn't want to go through the trouble of selling one place and buying another, but he wanted her out of that house.

He hadn't been straight with her about why, either, for fear he'd look like a jealous bastard. She'd shared the place with Jared, the creep who'd rejected her because she couldn't have a baby. She didn't belong in that house with whatever memories lingered there. She needed to start over. With him.

The possibility of that was fading as fast as the glow of her taillights through the rain. He had to step on it to keep up with her. She really should slow down.

She did put on the brakes as she approached the gravel section. If she got stuck he'd pull her out, and maybe that would give her time to reconsider leaving. He had to believe if they talked it out, if he could just hold her, this awful situation would improve.

But she drove through the gravel with no problem and continued down the road. He had no more reason to follow her except…she really was going too fast. Knowing she was so eager to get away from him cut like a knife.

Maybe once she'd driven for a while she'd settle down and reduce her speed. She wouldn't like it, but he'd follow her a little longer. He hoped he wouldn't push her to go faster.

But, damn it, the blacktop got slick as glass at times like this. She'd admitted that she wasn't used to the country. She lived in town, worked in town, probably didn't get out on the open road except to visit her folks in Laramie. He doubted she'd ever driven through a rainstorm at night.

Because he sat up higher than her sedan, he had a good view of the stretch of highway going past his turnoff. It was deserted. She braked the car again at the end of his road.

He wished she'd turn left, head back toward Thunder Mountain and spend the night there. If she did, he'd swing around and go back to Matt's. She'd be safe with Rosie and Herb.

Instead she turned right, toward the interstate. She sent up a spray of mud as she pulled onto the blacktop. He figured the mud had been aimed at him.

He wasn't close enough to get hit with it, but the gesture had been symbolic. She was done with him, completely done, and damned if he could figure out why. Her reaction to what he considered a reasonable suggestion was out of proportion.

That worried him more than anything. She'd pretended to be in control when she'd put on her clothes and left the house, but now that he thought about it, she'd been trembling. Her sudden decision to light out of there had thrown him for a loop and he hadn't paid as much attention as he should have.

Cautious behavior was her normal setting, but she wasn't being cautious tonight. As he kept up with her, he checked his speedometer. Holy moly. His truck was heavy enough that it wouldn't easily hydroplane, but her little sedan was—oh, God!

He jammed on the brakes and yelled as her car skidded off the road. His truck went into a spin, throwing him against the seat belt and coming to rest on the opposite shoulder. Leaping out, he ran across the empty two-lane highway.

Her car sat in a gully running thigh-deep with rain. His heartbeat was so loud he could barely hear the dark water churning past, but he could see it. His first instinct was to go down there, but he'd been in hard-rushing water before. He'd be no help to her if he got knocked off his feet first thing, and he would be.

He thought of the ropes in his truck. If he drove the truck over here, he could tie himself to the truck and work his way to her. Then she rolled down her window and he nearly passed out from relief. She hadn't been knocked unconscious by the impact…or worse.

He made a megaphone of his hands. "Are you okay?"

"Yes!" Her voice cracked a little but she didn't sound dazed. Scared, though. Real scared.

He decided on a different, quicker plan. "I'll get my rope!" He ran back across the highway. If a vehicle had come by, he'd have flagged it down, but it was late and nobody was out in this weather.

In his haste, he'd left his phone at home. Besides, by the time either of them called for help, he could have her out of there. He wasn't about to leave her sitting in that car any longer than necessary. The water could rise. A flash flood could come along.

A coil of rope over his shoulder and a pair of gloves in his back pocket, he dashed back to peer down at Tess. She faced him, her hands clutching the car door. He figured she was on her knees on the seat.

His vision narrowed until she was the only one in the frame. Tess. His Tess. He wouldn't let anything happen to her. Not as long as he had breath in his body. She was his joy.

The rain had let up a little so he didn't have to shout as loud. "I need you to climb out and straddle the window. Then I'll toss you this rope and you're going to

tighten it around your ribs and ease into the water. Then
I'll pull you up the bank. Got it?"

She nodded. Her face was white as she gazed at
him. She took a deep breath and hoisted herself out
the window.

"Hold up one arm. I'll aim for that." He'd never
roped in the rain, but he figured if he threw fast and
hard, that would help. He built the loop. He'd done it
millions of times, but this was the one that mattered.
"Coming at you."

The rope seemed to sail out in slow motion and he
stopped breathing as he watched it rise up and settle
down…right over her upheld arm. He sucked in a lungful of air and reached for the gloves in his back pocket.
"Okay. Now secure it under your arms and tighten it
real good."

She followed his instructions, although her move-
ments were jerky and once she wobbled as if she might
fall.

He broke out in a cold sweat. "Grip the door with
your legs as if you're riding a horse."

She nodded. After what seemed like forever, she
had the rope fastened under her arms. "Now what?"

"Bring your other leg out and slide down with your
back to me so you can hold on to the car as long as
possible. Then you'll have to let go and grab the rope
as you turn around. I'll keep it taut and gradually pull
you out of the water and up the bank. I'll go slow so I
don't jerk you off your feet."

"Zeke, what about your shoulder?"

"Lady, I don't give a damn about my shoulder.
Ready?"

"Ready."

He forced himself to breathe while she eased into the water. Before she turned around, he braced himself with both gloved hands on the rope. The rain had nearly stopped but the rope was still wet.

She stumbled once and he gasped. Then she got both hands on the rope and leaned back to snug up the line.

"Good! That's great. Just start walking as I pull you forward." He started the hand-over-hand motion in time with her steps and felt as if someone had jabbed a red-hot poker into his shoulder. Yep, he'd reinjured it. Oh, well.

He locked his gaze with hers and ignored the pain in his shoulder. "That's it. We're getting close. Watch out. Really slippery right there. Easy does it. Atta girl. A little more…little more…gotcha!" He pulled her into his arms and buried his face in her wet hair.

She clung to him and shook. "I thought…I might… die."

He hugged her tighter. "Not on my watch."

"Thank you, Zeke."

"You're welcome. Now, come on. Let's get you over to my truck." Moments later he sat in the passenger seat with Tess in his lap wrapped in a blanket he kept in the back of his cab. He'd turned the engine on and had the heat on low. He'd figure out what to do in a minute, but first he needed to just hold her.

She sighed and nestled against him. "Oh, Zeke, if you hadn't been here…"

"But I was. I had to be. I couldn't let anything happen to you."

"Or the baby."

That stunned him. "My God. I forgot all about the baby."

She lifted her head. The dim light from the dash revealed that her eyes were wide with surprise. "You forgot about the baby?"

"I know. Terrible, right? Probably wipes out all the points I've made so far regarding this kid."

"I didn't say that."

"No, but you could be thinking it." He sighed. "Tess, I can't deny it. When I saw you trapped in the car, I didn't think of anything but getting you to safety. I forgot you were pregnant. I forgot you hated my guts. Nothing mattered but saving you."

"I see." For some odd reason she was smiling.

That beautiful smile loosened his tongue some more. "You're my joy, Tess. The baby's wonderful, but when it comes right down to it, you're the one I…" He finally had to quit talking because his throat was becoming clogged.

Her voice was as soft as a caress. "The one you what, Zeke?"

He looked into eyes warm with happiness and shiny with tears. The words that had been lodged in his throat popped out. "I love you."

She burst into tears, but since she was hugging him like she'd never let him go, he thought her tears might not be a bad thing.

"Oh, Zeke," she wailed, her face pressed against his bare shoulder, the good one, fortunately. "I thought I'd never hear you say that."

He was shocked that he had. But those three words felt more right than any he'd ever spoken. He held her close and combed her wet hair with his fingers. "I'm not exactly used to saying it, to be honest. Matter of fact, I've never said that to another lady, not even Rosie."

Her words were thick with tears. "I had a hunch."

"But I can see now that it's the only thing that fits the situation. I love you. And if you have to live in Casper, okay, but please sell the house you used to live in with your ex."

She sniffed and looked up at him, her face damp from crying. "That bothers you?"

"Yes, ma'am."

"You know what? That house has never felt right to me but I hung on to it like a trophy and it really is perfect for a day care."

"But not the only one in the world, I'll bet."

"Definitely not. On the market it goes and, if I'm selling it, I might as well move to Sheridan."

He smiled with relief. "Thank you, sweet lady. You'll make lots of people happy with that decision, me included. Rosie and Herb will—" He caught himself. "Mom and Dad will love hearing it."

"I'm sure they will." The happy glow in her eyes told him that she realized what his slight correction meant.

Everything was going so well that he shouldn't push his luck, but then again, maybe this was the time to get it all out in the open. "As long as we're clearing the air, there's one more issue."

"Let me guess. You want us to get married."

"Yes, I surely do. I know it's a touchy subject but I need to give you fair warning. I'll probably keep asking even if it makes you mad."

"You could try asking me again right now."

"Yeah?"

She nodded.

His pulse rate kicked up a notch. "Well, then. Tess, will you marry me?"

"Yes."

"You *will*?" He could barely believe it. "Why?"

"Because I love *you* so much and finally, *finally*, I know that you love me back. If I had to end up in a ditch full of raging water before you could say it, then it was worth every terrifying second. I'd do it all again."

"Oh, God, don't say that." He cupped her cheek in one hand. "I hope I never go through another experience like that one."

She wrapped her arms around his neck and held his gaze. "I hate to break it to you, but loving someone means you probably will."

He sighed. "Then I hope it's a very long time before I go through such a moment again."

"I can't even promise you that much. Want to reconsider?"

"Not a chance." As he kissed her, he understood the full meaning of what his mom had told him. Exchanging risk for joy created a path to love. Because of Tess, he was the lucky guy who'd travel that path for the rest of his life.

Epilogue

The early morning flight from Auckland to LAX took eleven hours, so Austin Teague had booked an aisle seat to accommodate his six-foot, three-inch frame. He'd also managed to snag a spot in the two-seat section that ran along each side of the jumbo jet. Although he was still in economy, having only one other person sharing his space made it feel almost like business class.

He'd arrived first and, not long after, a pleasant-faced woman who looked to be in her sixties stopped in the aisle beside his seat. Her blond hair and rounded figure reminded him of his foster mom.

She smiled. "Looks like we'll be making this journey together." Her speech pegged her as being from the States, like him.

"Yes, ma'am." He got up and moved into the aisle

so she could take the window seat. She was carrying a large satchel stuffed with wrapped packages, probably souvenirs for the folks back home.

Instead of claiming her seat, she gazed up at him. "My, you are a tall, young man, aren't you?"

"Yes, ma'am. Can I hold your satchel for you while you slide in?"

"Actually, I have a much bigger favor to ask, but now that I see how tall you are, I probably shouldn't."

"What sort of favor, ma'am?"

"Well, um…" Her cheeks turned pink. "This is a long flight and I have a very small bladder. The aisle seats were all taken when I booked, so I was hoping to trade with the person I sat next to. But I can see you need room to stretch those long legs. I can't ask you to cram yourself into the window seat."

"Sure you can." He grabbed his duffel from under the seat in front of him and slid into the one next to the window. He shoved the duffel into its new home.

"Thank you *so* much. You're a lifesaver." She sat and reached into her satchel. "I picked this up on the Australian leg of my trip. I want you to have it." She handed him a boomerang-shaped package.

"I couldn't take this, ma'am." He smiled as he gave it back to her. "I'm sure you intend it for someone back home, someone who'll be mighty excited to get it."

"That may be true, but you just inconvenienced yourself for a stranger."

"Not at all. I was wondering if I'd made a mistake choosing the aisle. I like looking out."

"But we'll be flying over the Pacific. There's nothing to see except water."

"I like water." He'd be stuffed in this seat tighter

than a caterpillar in a cocoon, but she really did look like his foster mom. He couldn't deny someone who made him think of home and family.

"Then I'll accept your chivalrous offer. You may be glad of it in the long run. I'd be constantly asking you to get up so I could use the facilities."

"I'm glad it all worked out."

"Were you over here on vacation, too?"

"No, ma'am. I've been working near Queenstown as a trail guide."

"Hiking?"

He shook his head. "Horseback."

"I thought you looked like a cowboy! I was in Queenstown for a day. Took the tram up the side of the mountain, which was spectacular, but riding through that country would be something. Wasn't *Lord of the Rings* filmed in that area?"

"Yes, ma'am. We took folks to some of those locations. It's beautiful. I've spent the last four years making that ride and I never got tired of it."

"Well, now I want to come back."

"Then you should."

"I just might. I could write down the name of your company and ask for you personally."

He smiled. "Sorry, ma'am. I just quit my job and I'm heading home."

"Oh! You sounded so enthusiastic that I thought…" She seemed distressed. "I hope I didn't bring up an unpleasant subject."

"No, I loved it there. Seeing *Lord of the Rings* is what inspired me to save up so I could apply for the job. But someone close to me is getting married in

Wyoming. When I started thinking about going home for his wedding, I realized it was time to move back."

She sighed in obvious relief. "Well, then, good for you. Wyoming is beautiful, too. I've spent time in Yellowstone and Jackson Hole. Where are you from?"

"Sheridan."

"Never been there."

"It's not as well known as Jackson Hole, but there's nothing like waking up to the sun shining on the Bighorn Mountains. I've missed that." He hadn't wanted to admit he was homesick after all the effort he'd put into getting to Queenstown. New Zealand was amazing and the folks were friendly as all get-out. But the invitation to Cade and Lexi's wedding had made him realize he belonged in Wyoming.

"I'll bet the ladies in Sheridan will be pleased with your decision to come home."

He felt a blush coming on. "I don't know about that."

"Of course they will. You're handsome, personable and kind. Plus, you wouldn't even take that boomerang, which is hand-carved, by the way. Sure you won't change your mind?"

"Yes, ma'am, I'm sure." Time to switch topics. "Who's it for?"

"My oldest grandson. I have six grandchildren all together, four boys and two girls."

Austin started asking questions about her grandkids. He always got a kick out of listening to grandparents rave on about their grandchildren. His foster mom sent him constant updates on Sophie, and now another grandbaby was on the way.

He loved that Rosie had decided to claim the offspring of her foster boys as her grandkids. He looked forward to a time when he'd have a baby he could let Rosie spoil. The concept of a family of his own appealed to him more with every passing day.

Although he'd met some terrific women in New Zealand, they'd all had one drawback. They'd made it clear from the get-go that they wanted to stay put. If he'd grown up in Queenstown, he'd feel the same.

So he'd kept his relationships casual even as the urge to settle down had grown stronger. Lexi and Cade's wedding invitation had been the tipping point.

Finally it had dawned on him that if he wanted to build a future surrounded by his foster brothers and his foster parents, he needed to look for his life partner in Wyoming. He had a gut feeling she was there waiting for him. All he had to do was find her.

* * * * *

Another one of the THUNDER MOUNTAIN BROTHERHOOD *is heading home! Read Austin's story,* DO YOU TAKE THIS COWBOY? *coming August 2017 only from Harlequin Special Edition!*

Katrina Bailey's life is at a crossroads, so when arrogant—but sexy—Bowie Callahan asks for her help caring for his newly discovered half brother, she accepts, never expecting it to turn into something more...

Read on for a sneak peek at SERENITY HARBOR, the next book in the HAVEN POINT series by New York Times *bestselling author RaeAnne Thayne available July 2017!*

CHAPTER ONE

"THAT'S HIM AT your six o'clock, over by the tomatoes. Brown hair, blue eyes, ripped. Don't look. Isn't he *gorgeous*?"

Katrina Bailey barely restrained from rolling her eyes at her best friend. "How am I supposed to know that if you won't let me even sneak a peek at the man?" she asked Samantha Fremont.

Sam shrugged with another sidelong look in the man's direction. "Okay. You can look. Just make it subtle."

Mere months ago, all vital details about her best friend's latest crush might have been the most fascinating thing the two of them talked about all week. Right now, she found it tough to work up much interest in one more man in a long string of them, especially with everything else she had spinning in her life right now.

She wanted to ignore Sam's request and continue on with shopping for the things they needed to take to Wynona's shower—but friends didn't blow off their friends' obsessions. She loved Sam and had missed hanging out with her over the last nine months. It made her sad that their interests appeared to have diverged so dramatically, but it wouldn't hurt her to act like she cared about the cute newcomer to Haven Point.

Donning her best ninja spy skills—honed from

years of doing this very thing, checking out hot guys without them noticing—she pretended to reach up to grab a can of peas off the shelf. She studied the label intently, all while shifting her gaze toward the other end of the aisle.

About ten feet away, she spotted two men. Considering she knew Darwin Twitchell well—and he was close to eighty years old and cranky as a badger with gout—the other guy had to be Bowie Callahan, the new director of research and development at the Caine Tech facility in town.

Years of habit couldn't be overcome by sheer force of will. That was the only reason her stomach muscles seemed to shiver and her toes curled against the leather of her sandals. Or so she told herself, anyway.

Okay. She got it. Sam was totally right. The man was indeed great-looking: tall, lean, tanned, with sculpted features and brown hair streaked with the sort of blond highlights that didn't come from a salon but from spending time outside.

Under other circumstances, she might have wanted to do more than look. In a different life, perhaps she would have made her way to his end of the aisle, pretended to fumble with an item on the shelf, then dropped it right at his feet so they could "meet" while they both reached to pick it up.

She used to be such an idiot.

The old Katrina might not have been able to look away from such a gorgeous male specimen. But when he aimed a ferocious scowl downward, she shifted her gaze to find him frowning at a boy who looked to be about five or six, trying his best to put a box of sugary cereal into their cart and growing visibly upset when

Bowie Callahan kept taking it out and putting it back on the shelf.

Katrina frowned. "You didn't say he had a kid. I thought you had a strict rule. No divorced dads."

"He doesn't have a kid!" Sam exclaimed.

"Then who's the little kid currently winding up for what looks like a world-class tantrum at his feet?"

Ignoring her own stricture about not staring, Sam whirled around. Her eyes widened with confusion. "I have no idea! I heard it straight from Eliza Caine that he's not married and doesn't have a family. He never said anything to me about a kid when I met him at a party at Snow Angel Cove or the other two times I've bumped into him around town this spring. I haven't seen him around for a few weeks. Maybe he has family visiting. Or maybe he's babysitting or something."

That was so patently ridiculous, Katrina had to bite her tongue. Really? Did Sam honestly believe the new director of research and development at Caine Tech would be offering babysitting services—in the middle of the day and on a Monday, no less?

She sincerely adored Samantha for a million different reasons, but sometimes her friend saw what she wanted to see.

This latest example of how their paths had diverged in recent months made her a little sad. Until a year ago, she and Sam had been—as her mom would say—two peas of the same pod. They shared the same taste in music, movies, clothes. They could spend hours poring over celebrity and fashion magazines, dishing about the latest gossip, shopping for bargains at thrift stores and yard sales.

And men. She didn't even want to think about how

many hours of her life she had wasted with Sam, talking about whichever guy they were most interested in that day.

Samantha had been her best friend since they found each other in junior high in that mysterious way like discovered like.

She still loved her dearly. Sam was kind and generous and funny, but Katrina's own priorities had shifted. After the events of the last year, Katrina was beginning to realize she barely resembled the somewhat shallow, flighty girl she had been before she grabbed her passport and hopped on a plane with Carter Ross.

That was a good thing, she supposed, but she felt a little pang of fear that while on the path to gaining a little maturity, she might end up losing her best friend.

"Babysitting. I suppose it's possible," she said in a noncommittal voice. If so, the guy was really lousy at it. The boy's face had reddened, and tears had started streaming down his features. By all appearances, he was approaching a meltdown, and Bowie Callahan's scowl had shifted to a look of helpless frustration.

"If you want, I can introduce you," Sam said, apparently oblivious to the drama.

Katrina purposely pushed their cart forward, in the opposite direction. "You know, it doesn't look like a good time. I'm sure I'll have a chance to meet him later. I'll be in Haven Point for a month. Between Wyn's wedding and Lake Haven Days, there should be plenty of time to socialize with our newest resident."

"Are you sure?" Sam asked, disappointment clouding her gaze.

"Yeah. Let's just finish shopping so I have time to go home and change before the shower."

Not that her mother's house really felt like home anymore. Yet another radical change in the last nine months.

"I guess you're right," Sam said, after another surreptitious look over Katrina's shoulder. "We waited too long, anyway. Looks like he's moved to another aisle."

They found the items they needed and moved to the next aisle as well, but didn't bump into Bowie again. Maybe he had taken the boy, whoever he was, out of the store so he could cope with his meltdown in private.

They were nearly finished shopping when Sam's phone rang with the ominous tone she used to identify her mother.

She pulled the device out of her purse and glared at it. "I wish I dared to ignore her, but if I do, I'll hear about it for a week."

That was nothing, she thought. If Katrina ignored *her* mother's calls while she was in town for Wyn's wedding, Charlene would probably mount a search and rescue, which was kind of funny when she thought about it. Charlene hadn't been nearly as smothering when Kat had been living halfway around the world in primitive conditions for the last nine months. But if she dared show up late for dinner, sheer panic ensued.

"I'm at the grocery store with Kat," Samantha said, a crackly layer of irritation in her voice. "I texted you that's where I would be."

Her mother responded something Katrina couldn't hear, which made Sam roll her eyes. To others, Linda Fremont could be demanding and cranky, quick to criticize. Oddly, she had always treated Katrina with tolerance and even a measure of kindness.

"Do you absolutely need it tonight?" Samantha

asked, pausing a moment to listen to her mother's answer with obvious impatience written all over her features. "Fine. Yes. I can run over. I only wish you had
mentioned this earlier, when I was just hanging around
for three hours doing nothing, waiting for someone to
show up at the shop. I'll grab it."

She shut off her phone and shoved it back into her
little dangly Coach purse that she'd bought for a steal
at the Salvation Army in Boise. "I need to stop in next
door at the drugstore to pick up one of my mom's pre-
scriptions. Sorry. I know we're in a rush."

"No problem. I'll finish the shopping and check out,
then we can meet each other at your car when we're
done."

"Hey, I just had a great idea," Sam exclaimed. "After
the shower tonight, we should totally head up to Shelter Springs and grab a drink at the Painted Moose!"

Katrina tried not to groan. The last thing she wanted
to do amid her lingering jet lag was visit the local bar
scene, listening to the same songs, flirting with the
same losers, trying to laugh at their same old, tired
jokes.

"Let's play it by ear. We might be having so much
fun at the shower that we won't want to leave. Plus it's
Monday night, and I doubt there will be much going
on at the PM."

She didn't have the heart to tell Sam she wasn't the
same girl who loved nothing more than dancing with a
bunch of half-drunk cowboys—or that she had a feeling she would never be that girl again. Priorities had a
way of shifting when a person wasn't looking.

Sam stuck her bottom lip out in an exaggerated pout.

"Don't be such a party pooper! We've only got a month together, and I've missed you *so much*!"

Great. Like she needed more guilt in her life.

"Let's play it by ear. Go grab your mom's prescription, I'll check out and we'll head over to Julia's place. We can figure out our after-party plans, well, after the party."

She could tell by Sam's pout that she would have a hard time escaping a late night with her. Maybe she could talk her into just hanging out by the lakeshore and talking.

"Okay. I guess we'd better hurry if we want to have time to make our salad."

Sam hurried toward the front doors, and Katrina turned back to her list. Only the items from the vegetable aisle, then she would be done. She headed in that direction and spotted a flustered Bowie Callahan trying to keep the boy with him from eating grapes from the display.

"Stop it, Milo. I told you, you can eat as many as you want *after* we buy them."

This only seemed to make the boy more frustrated. She could see by his behavior and his repetitive mannerisms that he quite possibly had some sort of developmental issues. Autism, she would guess at a glance—though that could be a gross generalization, and she was not an expert, anyway.

Whatever the case, Callahan seemed wholly unprepared to deal with it. He hadn't taken the boy out of the store, obviously, to give him a break from the overstimulation. In fact, things seemed to have progressed from bad to worse.

Milo—cute name—reached for another grape despite the warning, and Bowie grabbed his hand and sternly looked down into his face. "I said, stop it. We'll have grapes after we pay for them."

The boy didn't like that. He wrenched his hand away and threw himself to the ground. "No! No! No!" he chanted.

"That's enough," Bowie Callahan snapped, loudly enough that other shoppers turned around to stare, which made the man flush.

She could see Milo was gearing up for a nuclear meltdown—and while she reminded herself it was none of her business, she couldn't escape a certain sense of professional obligation to step in.

She wanted to ignore it, to turn into the next aisle, finish her shopping and escape the store as quickly as she could. She could come up with a dozen excuses about why that was the best course of action. Samantha would be waiting for her. She didn't know the man or his frustrated kid. She had plenty of troubles of her own to worry about.

None of that held much weight when compared with the sight of a child, who clearly had some special needs, in great distress—and an adult who just as clearly didn't know what to do in the situation.

She felt an unexpected pang of sympathy for Bowie Callahan, probably because her mother had told her so many stories about how mortified Charlene would be when Katrina would have a seizure in a public place. All the staring, the pointing, the whispers.

The boy continued to chant "no" and began smacking his palm against his forehead in rhythm with each exclamation. A couple of older women she didn't know—tourists, probably—looked askance at the boy, and one muttered something to the other about how some children needed a swat on the behind.

She wanted to tell the old biddies to mind their own business but held her tongue, since she was about to ignore her own advice.

After another minute passed, when Bowie Callahan did nothing but gaze down at the boy with helpless frustration, Katrina knew she had to act. What other choice did she have? She pushed her cart closer. The man briefly met her gaze with a wariness that she chose to ignore. Instead, she plopped onto the ground next to the distressed boy.

In her experience with children of all ages and abilities, they reacted better to someone willing to lower to their level. She wasn't sure if he even noticed she was there, since he didn't stop chanting or smacking his palm against his head.

"Hi there." She spoke in a calm, conversational tone, as if she was chatting with one of her friends at Wynona's shower later in the evening. "What's your name?"

Milo—whose name she knew perfectly well from hearing Bowie use it—barely took a breath. "No! No! No! No!"

"Mine is Katrina," she went on. "Some people call me Kat. You know. Kitty-cat. Meow. Meow."

His voice hitched a little, and he lowered his hand but continued chanting, though he didn't sound quite as distressed. "No. No. No."

"Let me guess," she said. "Is your name Batman?" He frowned. "No. No. No."

"Is it… Anakin Skywalker?"

She picked the name, assuming by his Star Wars T-shirt it would be familiar to him. He shook his head. "No."

"What about Harry Potter?"

This time, he looked intrigued at the question, or perhaps at her stupidity. He shook his head.

"How about Milo?"

Big blue eyes widened with shock. "No," he said, though his tone gave the word the opposite meaning.

"Milo. Hi there. I like your name. I've never met anybody named Milo. Do you know anybody else named Kat?"

He shook his head.

"Neither do I," she admitted "But I have a cat. Her name is Marshmallow, because she's all white. Do you like marshmallows? The kind you eat, I mean."

He nodded and she smiled. "I do, too. Especially in hot cocoa."

He pantomimed petting a cat and pointed at her.

"You'd like to pet her? She would like that. She lives with my mom now and loves to have anyone pay attention to her. Do you have a cat or a dog, Milo?"

The boy's forehead furrowed, and he shook his head, glaring up at the man beside him, who looked stonily down at both of them.

Apparently that was a touchy subject.

Did the boy talk? She had heard him say only "no" so far. It wasn't uncommon for children on the autism spectrum and with other developmental delays to have much better receptive language skills than expressive skill, and he obviously understood and could get his response across fairly well without words.

"I see lots of delicious things in your cart—including cherries. Those are my favorite. Yum. I must have missed those. Where did you find them?"

He pointed to another area of the produce section,

where a gorgeous display of cherries gleamed under the fluorescent lights.

She pretended she didn't see them. Though the boy's tantrum had been averted for now, she didn't think it would hurt anything if she distracted him a little longer. "Do you think you could show me?"

It was a technique she frequently employed with her students who might be struggling, whether that was socially, emotionally or academically. She found that if she enlisted their help—either to assist her or to help out another student—they could often be distracted enough that they forgot whatever had upset them.

Milo craned his neck to look up at Bowie Callahan for permission. The man looked down at both of them, a baffled look on his features, but after a moment he shrugged and reached a hand down to help her off the floor.

She didn't need assistance, but it would probably seem rude to ignore him. She placed her hand in his and found it warm and solid and much more calloused than a computer nerd should have. She tried not to pay attention to the little shock of electricity between them or the tug at her nerves.

"Thanks," she mumbled, looking quickly away as she followed the boy, who, she was happy to notice, seemed to have completely forgotten his frustration.

Don't miss SERENITY HARBOR
by RaeAnne Thayne
available wherever HQN books and ebooks are sold!

Copyright © 2017 by RaeAnne Thayne

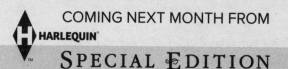

COMING NEXT MONTH FROM

HARLEQUIN®

SPECIAL EDITION

Available July 18, 2017

#2563 MOMMY AND THE MAVERICK
Montana Mavericks: The Great Family Roundup
by Meg Maxwell
Billionaire businessman Autry Jones swore off single mothers after enduring the pain of losing both the woman he loved *and* her child when she dumped him. That is, until he meets widowed mother of three Marissa Jones, who changes his mind—and his life—in three weeks.

#2564 DO YOU TAKE THIS COWBOY?
Thunder Mountain Brotherhood • by Vicki Lewis Thompson
Recently returned to Wyoming from New Zealand, Austin Teague is determined to find a wife and settle down. But he manages to fall hard for the fiercely independent Drew Martinelli, the one woman who's dead set against getting married.

#2565 HOW TO TRAIN A COWBOY
Texas Rescue • by Caro Carson
Benjamin Graham is a former marine, not a cowboy. So when he gets a job as a ranch hand, he has a lot to learn. Luckily, Emily Davis is willing to teach him everything he needs to know. But as the attraction between them grows, Graham and Emily will both have to face their pasts and learn to embrace the future.

#2566 VEGAS WEDDING, WEAVER BRIDE
Return to the Double C • by Allison Leigh
It looks like Penny Garner and Quinn Templeton had a Vegas wedding when they wake up in bed together with rings and a marriage certificate. While they put off a divorce to determine if she's pregnant, can Quinn convince Penny to leave her old heartbreak in the past and become his Weaver bride?

#2567 THE RANCHER'S UNEXPECTED FAMILY
The Cedar River Cowboys • by Helen Lacey
Helping Cole Quartermaine reconnect with his daughter was all Ash McCune intended to do. Falling for the sexy single dad was not part of the plan. But plans, she quickly discovers, have a way of changing!

#2568 AWOL BRIDE
Camden Family Secrets • by Victoria Pade
After a car accident leaves runaway bride Maicy Clark unconscious, she's rescued by the last man on earth she ever wanted to see again:
Conor Madison, her high school sweetheart, who rejected her eighteen years ago. And if that isn't bad enough, she's stranded in a log cabin with him, in the middle of a raging blizzard, with nothing to do but remember just how good they were together.

YOU CAN FIND MORE INFORMATION ON UPCOMING HARLEQUIN® TITLES,
FREE EXCERPTS AND MORE AT WWW.HARLEQUIN.COM.

HSECNM0717

Get 2 Free Books,
Plus 2 Free Gifts—
just for trying the
Reader Service!

HARLEQUIN®

SPECIAL EDITION

YES! Please send me 2 FREE Harlequin® Special Edition novels and my 2 FREE gifts (gifts are worth about $10 retail). After receiving them, if I don't wish to receive any more books, I can return the shipping statement marked "cancel." If I don't cancel, I will receive 6 brand-new novels every month and be billed just $4.99 per book in the U.S. or $5.74 per book in Canada. That's a savings of at least 12% off the cover price! It's quite a bargain! Shipping and handling is just 50¢ per book in the U.S. and 75¢ per book in Canada.* I understand that accepting the 2 free books and gifts places me under no obligation to buy anything. I can always return a shipment and cancel at any time. The free books and gifts are mine to keep no matter what I decide.

235/335 HDN GLWR

Name _____ (PLEASE PRINT)

Address _____ Apt. #

City _____ State/Province _____ Zip/Postal Code

Signature (if under 18, a parent or guardian must sign)

Mail to the **Reader Service:**
IN U.S.A.: P.O. Box 1341, Buffalo, NY 14240-8531
IN CANADA: P.O. Box 603, Fort Erie, Ontario L2A 5X3

Want to try two free books from another line?
Call 1-800-873-8635 or visit www.ReaderService.com.

*Terms and prices subject to change without notice. Prices do not include applicable taxes. Sales tax applicable in N.Y. Canadian residents will be charged applicable taxes. Offer not valid in Quebec. This offer is limited to one order per household. Books received may not be as shown. Not valid for current subscribers to Harlequin Special Edition books. All orders subject to approval. Credit or debit balances in a customer's account(s) may be offset by any other outstanding balance owed by or to the customer. Please allow 4 to 6 weeks for delivery. Offer available while quantities last.

Your Privacy—The Reader Service is committed to protecting your privacy. Our Privacy Policy is available online at www.ReaderService.com or upon request from the Reader Service.

We make a portion of our mailing list available to reputable third parties that offer products we believe may interest you. If you prefer that we not exchange your name with third parties, or if you wish to clarify or modify your communication preferences, please visit us at www.ReaderService.com/consumerschoice or write to us at Reader Service Preference Service, P.O. Box 9062, Buffalo, NY 14240-9062. Include your complete name and address.

HSE17R2

SPECIAL EXCERPT FROM

H HARLEQUIN®

SPECIAL EDITION

*Billionaire businessman Autry Jones swore off single
mothers—until he meets widowed mom of three
Marissa Jones just weeks before he's supposed to leave
for a job in Paris...*

Read on for a sneak preview of
MOMMY AND THE MAVERICK
by **Meg Maxwell**, *the second book in the*
MONTANA MAVERICKS: THE GREAT FAMILY
ROUNDUP *continuity.*

"Right. We shook on being friends. But..." She paused and dropped down onto the love seat across from the fireplace.

"But things feel more than friendly between us," he finished for her. "There was that kiss, for one. And the fact that every time I see you I want to kiss you again."

"Ditto. See the problem?"

He smiled and sat down beside her. "Marissa, why did you come here? To tell me that doing the competition with Abby is a bad idea? That she's going to get too attached to me?"

"Yup."

"Except you didn't say that."

"Because I don't want to take it from her. I want her to be excited about the competition. To not lose out on something when she's been dealt a hard blow in life so young. But yeah, I am worried she's going to get too attached. All three girls. But especially Abby."

"Abby knows I'm leaving for Paris at the end of August. That's a given. Goodbye is already in the air, Marissa. We're not fooling anyone."

"Why do I keep fighting it, then?" she asked. "Why do I have to keep reminding myself that feeling the way I do about you is only going to—"

"Make you feel like crap when I go? I know. I've had that same talk with myself fifty times. I wasn't expecting to meet you, Marissa. Or want you so damned bad every time I see you."

It wasn't just about sex, but he wasn't putting that out there. If she kept it to sexual attraction, surface stuff, maybe he'd believe it. Then he could enjoy his time with Marissa and go in a couple weeks without much strain in his chest.

"So what do we do?" she asked. "Give in to this or be smart and stay nice and platonic?"

He reached for her hand. "I don't know."

"Your hair's still damp," she said. "I can smell your shampoo. And your soap."

He leaned closer and kissed her, his hands slipping around her shoulders, down her back, drawing her to him. He felt her stiffen for a second and then relax. "I don't want to just be friends, Marissa. I want you."

She kissed him back, her hands in his hair, and he could feel her breasts against his chest. He sucked in a breath, overwhelmed by desire, by need. "You're sure?" he asked, pulling back a bit to look at her, directly into her beautiful dark brown eyes.

"No, I'm not sure," she whispered. "I just know that I want you, too."

Don't miss
MOMMY AND THE MAVERICK by Meg Maxwell,
available August 2017 wherever
Harlequin® Special Edition books and ebooks are sold.

www.Harlequin.com

Copyright © 2017 by Harlequin Books S.A.

HSEEXP0717

EXCLUSIVE LIMITED TIME OFFER AT
www.HARLEQUIN.com

$7.99 U.S./$9.99 CAN.

$1.⁰⁰ OFF

New York Times Bestselling Author

RaeAnne
Thayne

*In the town of Haven Point,
love can be just a wish—and one
magical kiss—away...*

SERENITY
HARBOR

*Available June 27, 2017
Get your copy today!*

Receive **$1.00 OFF** the purchase price of
SERENITY HARBOR by RaeAnne Thayne
when you use the coupon code below on Harlequin.com.

SERENITY1

Offer valid from June 27, 2017, until July 31, 2017, on www.Harlequin.com.

Valid in the U.S.A. and Canada only. To redeem this offer, please add the print or
ebook version of SERENITY HARBOR by RaeAnne Thayne to your shopping cart
and then enter the coupon code at checkout.

DISCLAIMER: Offer valid on the print or ebook version of SERENITY HARBOR
by RaeAnne Thayne from June 27, 2017, at 12:01 a.m. ET until July 31, 2017,
11:59 p.m. ET at www.Harlequin.com only. The Customer will receive $1.00 OFF
the list price of SERENITY HARBOR by RaeAnne Thayne in print or ebook on
www.Harlequin.com with the **SERENITY1** coupon code. Sales tax applied where
applicable. Quantities are limited. Valid in the U.S.A. and Canada only. All orders
subject to approval.

® and ™ are trademarks owned and used by the trademark owner and/or its licensee.
© 2017 Harlequin Enterprises Limited

HQN™
www.HQNBooks.com

PHCOUPRATSE0717

Earn points from all your Harlequin book purchases from wherever you shop.

Turn your points into *FREE BOOKS* of your choice
OR
EXCLUSIVE GIFTS from your favorite
authors or series.

Join for FREE today at
www.HarlequinMyRewards.com.

Harlequin My Rewards is a free program (no fees) without any commitments or obligations.

MYR17

THE WORLD IS BETTER
WITH
Romance

Harlequin has everything from contemporary, passionate and heartwarming to suspenseful and inspirational stories.

Whatever your mood, we have a romance just for you!

Connect with us to find your next great read, special offers and more.

f /HarlequinBooks

🐦 @HarlequinBooks

www.HarlequinBlog.com

www.Harlequin.com/Newsletters

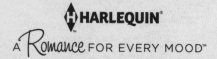

◆ HARLEQUIN®

A *Romance* FOR EVERY MOOD™

www.Harlequin.com

SERIESHALOAD2015